Real to Reel

Real to Reel
Lidia Yuknavitch

FC2
Normal / Tallahassee

Published by FC2 with support provided by Florida State University,
the Unit for Contemporary Literature of the Department of English at
Illinois State University, the Program for Writers of the Department of
English of the University of Illinois at Chicago, the Illinois Arts Council,
and the Florida Arts Council of the Florida Division of Cultural Affairs

Address all inquiries to: Fiction Collective Two, Florida State University,
c/o English Department, Tallahassee, FL 32306-1580

ISBN: Paper, 1-57366-107-4

Library of Congress Cataloging-in-Publication Data
Yuknavitch, Lidia.
    Real to reel : short fictions / by Lidia Yuknavitch.— 1st ed.
        p. cm.
    ISBN 1-57366-107-4   3003/222   1/04
1. United States—Social life and customs—21st century—Fiction. I.
Title.
    PS3575.U35 R43 2003
    813'.54--dc21
                                        2002012646

Cover Design: Victor Mingovits
Book Design: Lisa Savage and Tara Reeser

Illinois ARTS Council
AN AGENCY OF
THE STATE OF ILLINOIS

This program is
partially supported
by a grant from the
Illinois Arts Council

FLORIDA Arts

This book is for Andy Mingo

The following stories have appeared previously:

"Scripted" in *New American Letters*
"Male Lead" in *Black Ice*
"Shooting" in *Fiction International*
"Chair" in *Exquisite Corpse*
"Beatings" was performed as a filmic narrative at the word festival
sponsored by 2 gyrlz productions

Deepest thanks to Cris Mazza, Tara Reeser, Brenda Mills, Ralph
Berry, and Lance Olsen, without whose help these words would
not live. You move me.

Content is a glimpse of something. It is very tiny, content.
—Willem de Kooning

The moving image arrests its viewer inside motion; from this vantage we experience frames and bits and pieces of things as if they were fluid.
—Jackson Pollock

How weirdly reality moves.
—David Lynch

History is a pile of ruins...image upon image...wreckage.
—Walter Benjamin

There are other stories, there are other ways of telling. The body of a woman might yield a new foreign language.
—Marguerite Duras

contents

Scripted

I am not myself. It seems some slippage has occurred. I am not exactly sure when, but I suspect it began just under a year ago, perhaps closer to two. In some ways the slipping might be attributed to the normal flow of events. Changes in one's life, for example, function rather simplistically in this way, and I have never been one to be thrown or alarmed by what appear to be movements completely in line with ordinary or even cosmic patterns. Aging, seasons and tides, the way consciousness or wisdom changes the structure of things. The way thought rescues us from action time and again.

She is not herself. It feels as if someone has sliced open her belly and is reaching inside. She closes her eyes. She places her hands—one under each lower rib—and pulls. Like a surgeon's tool. This is what it feels like to be her. And yet she does not count this as damaging or traumatic or depressing or terrifying; somehow this seems the natural order of things, like an animal shedding its skin or something dying giving way to new life. Bees swarming out of the carcass of a cow— isn't that how Virgil made spring happen from all that death? Poetry saves us. Words give us the ability to move.

You are not yourself, and what's worse, you know it. It's been clear to you for some time, though you seem to have hoodwinked friends, colleagues, ordinary people such as grocery store clerks, gas station attendants, and waitresses. You exchange money and goods and services in the usual way, you arrive and depart as always, but secretly you know that these are acts of extreme stealth. At first you had some concern that someone would notice, as if you were carrying around a wound, but as time passed it became obvious that no one at all noticed, and wouldn't. Ever. In fact, you could be anyone.

After all. I am old enough now to have a vantage point from which to view the story, so to speak, of a life. I can see plots, turns, echoes, the recurrence of main and subordinate characters, tensions, conflicts, resolutions, and epiphanies all in perfect little rows. Some no doubt would identify this as a kind of wisdom. However, something nags at me in the back of my head like a small worm burrowing through my skull. It says: this is not so. In other words I am struck with the feeling that I am entirely deluded at the very point at which this mythological wisdom is presenting itself. The tunnel that the little worm has dug reveals a vacant tube of ignorance. The vantage point moves. It is a blur of pure motion, thus, invisible.

After all, she has been moved by a single line, a page, she has been literally moved. Once at a bar drinking scotch she seized-up mid-sip, the scotch dribbling down her lip and chin; the words, a poet's; her mind, convulsing; her body, a plethora of blood and channels of vein like worm colonies mapping out whole new geographies. The line had so overtaken her that she had walked directly out into the street into the rain and the night and stood there until she had been entirely soaked, looking out into space, into the street itself, the black and white schemata of night, knowing with perfect certainty that she had to leave that city and go to another, without cause or effect, without reason, syntax, or insight. It was simply the line moving her.

After all, you don't give a flying crap about any of the people that people your life, now do you? Their inane and idle chatter and petty microscopic concerns. Their crawling through their own lives like blind earthworms in a clod of dirt no bigger than a baseball diamond. Their overwrought pathos and their absurd, tiny victories. They are cartoons of themselves. Their needs don't just bore the shit out of you, they actually repulse you. The way they proclaim insight from bogus interpretations of little events in their lives. Or how they are moved by great works of art and questions of being. A pile of steaming shit is what you really think even as you move through lively dinner conversations, attend concerts, go to funerals. You immovable fuck.

Spinning in this way, I try to track what's what. As near as I can determine, this slippage of self may have a cause and effect relationship, or a kind of fated fall motif (you know,

Spinning in this way she enters a new city again or for the first time. Her clothes change, her hair, her creature comforts, what moves her, everything reinvented. She

Spinning in this cesspool called a melting pot you wonder what's the use of this idiotic farce called democracy, and your place in it as an individual, the whole the adage that there are no accidents…) or even an Eastern metaphysical shape, but it seems equally possible that the entire falling is accidental, without cause, effect, or meaning. It's not as if building a self over the course of one's life is tantamount to designing and constructing a building, now is it? In that architecture such systems and equations drive the movement that one cannot at any point step back and extract oneself from the matrix of its meaning. Conversely, a life, though we see it as designed (through our own consciousness or larger than ourselves), is.

takes up philosophy not as hobby but as obsession. Finds herself inside books palm side up, Kant and Hegel, Wittgenstein. The words so moving at times her head rocks back. Secretly she reads Simone Weil, *Lives of the Saints*; their ecstasies keep moving her to ask, where are the bodies? She reads phenomenology thinking it will track the corporeal but finds that she is wrong. Sometimes it helps her to read direct medical descriptions of death, so the ideas that lift her in that transcendent way are always tethered to the ground of a human corpse.

social organization of human culture into capitalist segments. Like chocolates in a box, prison cells, office cubicles. Lines at restaurants and museums, like cattle, like food in jars and cans and boxes. Like knowledge alphabetized and stacked, burned onto computer disks, kept safe from expansion by ever wily forms of containment feigning systemization. Even the sky is charted, the human body. Ranges of emotions and psychologies. Money. God. What a punk, you think. How a whole culture can be tricked by clever stories, movies, and mappings.

Take Wittgenstein: "The flashing of an aspect of being seems half visual experience, half thought." Unlike artistic forms, being, to put it simply, wavers. Where art is open to interpretation, being is open to dissolution. The two cross paths however at the interstices of making and of signification; each thrusts its meaning forward toward an

Take Joan of Arc. She can see the image of her death. The details move her. The written account by Vita Sackville-West: "The sulfur was lit and the top layers of skin burned away; a faint honey smell was recorded." And Falconetti. In the silent black and white film. Her face is the word for it. Artaud's mad longing, his

Take technology. Do you know what happens if you type "being" into a search engine? Try it. Try Yahoo or Google. (First take a moment to think about the words "search engine," "yahoo," and "google." These are our knowledge bases. No shit). Since nearly every person you know is a lazy ass, you withdraw the other and in that relationship we come to "know" or experience. And history, personal as well as cultural, derives from just these relationships. So in the case of Wittgenstein then we are speaking about being not as transcendent of meaning (as in god), but rather tethered, forever grounded, to the process of sight and insight. So my own slippage of self in this regard might be said to represent this fluctuation.

desire mixing with sacrament like blood and dirt from wounds in battle. These speak to her. Inside these words and images a body comes alive, faith made corporeal in wounding and even death. Love. She can make herself dizzy simply by thinking of it. She could probably faint right now if she let herself. Certainly she has been moved to tears publicly and endlessly simply by the named thing.

projection of the question. In your own mind you answer it: "crockofshit" comes up. The total tonnage of perfect shit—but accurate about us, nonetheless—that this represents to you is enough to fill a stadium. Being. Now that's a good one. Breathing, eating, shitting, eating, fucking. You would not even include thinking in the list. Descartes. What kind of asshole thinks that piece of crap up?

Making meaning, however, has its tricks. Part of how we most acutely make meaning of the events in our lives is theological in nature. I do not mean to say that we are yet bound to old notions of god and heaven. But we are still bound to their forms. For instance, when we hit any kind of difficulty or crisis, the first impulse of course is to narrativize, to make a story out of the event, a story complete with sin and redemption, moral trial and condemnation, transcendence, forgiveness,

The meaning of things makes her. What moves her, makes her. In this way she becomes exactly what she is reading, she becomes Wittgenstein's line, she becomes Falconetti's face, she becomes a description of burning flesh. In slow walks down city streets into bars she is pale and lonesome, so pale and lonesome someone is always moved to ask her why she is so sad, exactly as in a movie or novel, exactly like the constellation of a philosophy answering the question, what is a woman, she becomes the

Why not make it up? Make up a version of things since no one will notice anyway. The colossal stupidity of your fellow man will make it simple. Someone asks you your name, make one up. See what changes. Someone asks you what you do for a living, if you are married, have children, what your age is, your income, what kind of car you drive, where you are from—fictionalize it all. You think it will make a difference but it won't make the kind of difference you are hoping that it will. Instead of and resurrection. We take our emotions and make story from biblical form, from The Story, as it were. Thus all our smaller stories carry with them the plot elements of The Story: suffering, anguish, punishment, transcendence.... Do you see?

embodiment of the knowledge to the point of near iconography. Seated at a table drinking she places a hand to her cheek and the other at her collarbone, she closes her eyes, she is seeing lines and lines.... Can you see her?

stunning or changing or warping anything in your life, it will simply make people more interested in the person you are describing than they were in you. There is absolutely no distance between blindness and insight.

I will give you an example. A small and familiar human drama. Let's say a man cheats on his wife with a younger woman. Let's say the man and the wife's relationship, over time and with ordinary inevitability, has become rote. Not necessarily cold or sterile, not without love, not even without compassion. But habitual. The ease with which the man leans into the younger woman is based on another old story; she is attracted by his wisdom, or what she perceives to be his wisdom. He doesn't even have to do anything but look her way, pay attention to her. He need only be older and wiser than the young woman. Who is of course, beautiful.

She is an example of the thing itself. She has been betrayed, scorned, shamed. A lover takes her, she falls. Then, inevitable, disgusted with her mind, with its complications and little weavings, with her constant weeping and overdramatic scenes, her cerebral contortions, turns her out either verbally or physically or emotionally. He either returns to his wife or former lover, or he gains self-worth and insight from their encounter; what it revealed to him about himself, his vulnerabilities, his being and purpose in life. First she is broken. And then she is simply a self again, but without ownership of any sort, she is simply a self set

Look at these lame idiots, you think. Are they not repeating the same goddamn piece of shit story that all of pukey humanity has Xeroxed since the dawn of time, you think. Some middle-aged fuck needing to fuck some empty need-machine of youth who didn't get proper daddy or who is just generally let down by this culture's available roles for being— women, who can blame them for being pissed and insane— her mouth endlessly open, her tears neverending, his moronic lunging even though his nut-sack is sagging and his life's worth is wrinkled and gray and about the only thing he can point to and say this exists is his wife at home with her own deflated blown-

Already the setting, characters, conflict, and resolution are clear, yes?

sailing across a sea of signifiers as if lifted from the pages of a story.

out balloons for tits…stop me when this story sounds FAMILIAR.

You don't have to have read any canon to comprehend the idea here. You need only to have lived a life, subjected yourself to a culture's discourses. You need only to have been alive. These stories have supersaturated being, so to speak, and so they are no longer jettisoned away from us, they are in us, as in us as DNA, as close to us as skin. It does not matter what one chooses or doesn't choose in a life. Certain stories override any will you may or may not have. Certain stories write us. If you doubt what I am speaking of, make a list of the last five movies or books or songs or news stories which moved you. I suggest to you that each will have one thing in common. Each will draw from a very short list of pre-existing scripts.

Books are not people. She knows that. And yet don't all of the people who people her life behave exactly as she has read? She has a private thought which is "all being is textual." She knows now not to tell anyone this thought. She keeps lines such as this inside of a dialogue never uttered. Her lines thus correspond with lines she has read in a complex discussion without beginning, middle, or end. Without primary characters or directed action. Just lines in the mind of one woman. She knows now that if someone speaks to her she ought to respond not with any of these lines, but with pre-coded body-specific phrases, like sound-bites or authorized advertisements. Someone says are you from here. Animal instinct-like she knows to say yes.

Fuck literature. I mean let's be real. We don't need it anymore. I say get rid of all the books since no one, anywhere, has the patience or time to read them anymore. Yeah, I know some of you out there will CLAIM that you are a reader of texts, that you read every word from beginning to end, but I say you are full of shit. You know how many academics I know that get away with reading the back jacket of a book instead of its contents? Let's just say a lot. Because what matters is that they can talk the talk, not that they have read something in its entirety. What matters is that they can tell a story of experience. The experience itself, of a book, of a life, it doesn't matter—everybody has already done and heard everything enough to puke.

So the man and the woman fall to desire, or the story of a desire which entirely always already contains them. So too they exit that story with experiences which will no doubt shape their futures. Perhaps the man goes back to his wife, or divorces his wife and marries the younger woman, only to have another affair five years later. Perhaps the woman moves to the city in which the man lives, takes up a life with him, takes on his life as her narration. However, there are two interpretations here. Either the experience of desire changes them and influences their future actions or decisions, or the experience of desire neither changes nor influences them at all and is itself merely a nexus within which we dip in and out as individuals. Like a universe.

Yes she says to a man. To men. Any men. Yes like a serial. Yes to a desire without origin, without specific bodies, and yet located in her flesh perpetually. Yes to a future, as long as each future posits and then erases itself forever. Yes to a husband, a new city, yes to being, as long as being always posits itself and then erases itself forever. Yes to all of language, to all cities, all names, to open mouths and legs. Yes to life in Paris, in Seattle, in Los Angeles, New York, Berlin, Texas. Yes to metamorphosis, catharsis, epiphany, transcendence. Yes to the order inside of chaos, the moving particles underneath what appears to be immovable skin, yes to the entire nebula, to the entire night sky, to the endless cosmos.

Open your mouth and eat shit. What I'm saying is every single time someone speaks their mind you are, in effect, eating shit. Their shit. What's more, every time you open your own mouth you are spewing shit. The entire human race is idle chatter. North America, chatter. Europe, chatter with an accent. Africa and other third world victimized poor little boobies scrounging around for food or governments, nations, blah blah blah blah blah blah shit. Men and women, worse than excrement. Ask yourself this: are we better than we used to be together? Men and women? Have things improved in ways that you can point to and feel good about? How? What do you do in your little cosmology with race class gender? You punk.

And so the end of this point. I did not mean to imply that I had an answer, either for myself, or in the form of advice for a reader. I meant

Her telos has become beloved to her. She thinks this sentence as a man is coming inside of her. She does not speak it. She moans in the

I don't have anything else to say. You'll reject all this crap anyway, right? You fucking "reader" of other people's ideas. You can merely to raise the question. In my individual case the question came to be about being, an old question, I admit, perhaps a dull one to some. I am not so much interested in whether or not I am, but rather, how I am. And certainly phenomenology, epistemology, ontology all rake through the chaos of that. But my "how" is embedded with perhaps a more subtle and urgent question…a question I would leave with you, reader, as Keats leaving his hand, open and extended: this living, isn't it simply to be storied?

voice of a woman in ecstasy. He is pleased. Her telos, secret, private, entirely an ecstatic state, will be that which is closest to death. The last page. The last sentence. The last image. The last word, letter. The silence which comes then. Alive and unflinching and nearly unbearable, the space wherein one is compelled to find the next book, film, lover, event, life, self. Hurry, they all think. She thinks, die die die die die die in a loop. She smiles. He smiles back. Two lovers fucking. It is the way of the world. It is every story ever told, and she inhabits them all.

simply say, this asshole is full of shit, wrongheaded, uneducated, biased, crass, mistaken, misguided, full of themselves, confused, high, nuts, immoral, damaged, imbecilic, delusional, without a grasp of basic humanity or language or being or community or social processes or human history or knowledge or order or science or law or cultural production or awareness or love…the stupidest of all…love…what the fuck do we know about love? Love doesn't know from Adam. Don't bother thinking or being. Don't bother moving. Get real.

Male Lead

(as narrated by Keanu Reeves during an "Inside the Actors Studio" interview)

This book I read, well, it's one that, no shit, changed my life. I know everybody says that kind of thing. This or that movie, this or that book, this or that song changed my life. It's a cliché, is what I'm saying. I know that. For sure. But what I'm saying is that this book really did change the shape, direction, and movement of my entire life. Hold on. I know what you're thinking. That guy, he's full of shit. He's just being overdramatic or self-important or some other kind of crap. But I'm telling you. If you just give me a chance, I can explain. You'll see. You'll see it all.

I'm not saying I'm old or anything, but I'm at a place in my life where I can, you know, look back at things. For the first time. I mean, I'm halfway through my thirties already. Forty's just around the corner, you know what I'm saying? And I've got this…well, sort of different sense of my life. I can see patterns and shit. I can see shapes and the past as a kind of story type deal. So that means I can also see the parts that are more meaningful. And you know what the pisser is? It's not the stuff you thought was important when it was happening. The stuff you thought was the crisis. It's the stuff you thought was no big whoop that turns out carried all the importance. I think you know what I'm saying. Maybe not exactly, but pretty much you do, don't you?

Keanu the actor stops speaking momentarily and looks a little off into space. It's almost as if he's pausing to smoke, only the actor isn't smoking. As we've seen from several of his movies, he's not a very convincing smoker. He has this extraordinarily blank look on his face that it is quite possible only he can achieve. In fact this may be his true gift, his singular brilliance as an actor. That sort of "stunned to the point of drooling" look.

Keanu the man, on the other hand, is feeling self-conscious as hell. He's having that old feeling he's had so many times before. The one that goes, what the fuck. What the fuck. Why am I doing this? Who are these people? This is the stupidest thing in the world. This is more stupid than sitting on your own toilet taking an enormous crap while drilling your own fucking nose.

The audience is filled with students. They are there to learn. Some of them feel lucky as crap to be there, such an accomplished actor, not old and out of touch but right there in it, man, living it. They just want to soak up what the man has to say. Others are more skeptical, they are waiting for profundity to reveal itself, or if not profundity, just something they can make direct and speedy use of. I'd be lying to you if I said that was everyone. There are also some students in the audience who think Keanu Reeves is an idiot, that he can't act his way out of a paper bag. Pretty much the only reason they came was to go drink later and make up one-acts spoofing Keanu Reeves' every move, every word, every gesture. They think it's a sorry-ass racket when this Hollywood hack-of-a-loser no-talent stoner can make it. And yes, they've heard Dogstar and it only confirmed their suspicions. They think things like Keanu Reeves is like Johnny Depp's retarded inbred cousin. They think things like this class is a waste of time. They think things like good thing we're stoned or this whole afternoon would be a bust.

The actor continues.

I mean, it's the weirdest goddamn thing, but art can truly change your life. I'm living proof. Case in point. Have you noticed that every movie Brad Pitt has made since he did *Fight Club*, he's just repeating the same character, the same mannerisms, the same movements? It's that book, that *Fight Club* book by that Palachuck guy...

Someone from the audience corrects him—Palahniuk. Chuck Palahniuk.

...yeah. That guy. Whatever. I heard Pitt fucking loved that book, that he thanked that guy that wrote it in the middle of filming a scene. I mean, that book changed his life, since it changed him as an actor.

What?

Someone from the audience asks Keanu Reeves what book he's read that has changed his life.

Oh, I don't remember right now. All's I'm saying is you have to read literature. You have to get back in touch with stories and characters...that's where the art of it is.

In the audience, at least one woman's twat is itching. Even some of the guys' crotches twitch. I mean, he's a good-looking motherfucker, in that sort of Alaskan white boy kind of way. Remember the guy that played Ed on "Northern Exposure?" Either somewhat Alaskan, or partially Japanese or Pacific Asian.... He kind of has that look only more *GQ*. Right? So lots of the people in the audience are horny is what I'm saying.

There is also, however, a guy from Seattle with an MFA in fiction writing and a couple of published novels. He's smoking. He smokes like a guy who could be filmed smoking. The smoke barely escapes his parted lips, and he doesn't squint or blow the smoke away. You know what I'm saying. And his hand doesn't look like a guy trying to hold a cigarette. It just looks like his hand's supposed to look. With the cigarette. Total screen success. He's pretty much Gaped out

in his look, from Brooks Brothers' glasses to fitted matte
black jersey long-sleeved T to stone-washed khakis to black
relaxed leather zip on the side sort of bourgeois leisure shoes.
But his consumerism and name-brand exterior pales in com-
parison to the Keanu effect—some mix of Urban Outfitters/
used Puma pretend poverty/Saks Fifth Avenue—and thus
he looks rather minimalist next to Keanu. Classier than Keanu
is what I'm saying. Less like an actor.

This guy is sitting there going jesus god, what a fuck.
What a pretentious, clownish fuck. How does this *asshole*
do it? I can see how he may have gotten his foot in the door,
but christ, after he'd been around a while, opening his mouth
and saying these kinds of things, didn't anyone notice? This
guy decides right then and there that he will make a movie
parodying Keanu Reeves in which a guy acting like Keanu
Reeves plays James T. Kirk in a "Star Trek" episode where
the aliens are books. Telepathic, bodiless, books.

Two rows back, one seat over. Her tiny shoulders. Her
edged white face. Her ribs like those of a bird's. Black as a
record album hair, tinted blue. She is so sharp and tight she
is like quicksilver. As fast as shutter speed or clicking light.
She has the kind of breathing that rushes to that place just
under the throat. Her lungs keep it up there. Her eyes barely
hold in their little sockets. They stutter from head to head.
She can see words in the air around everyone, singing up
then sputtering out like ashes from a fire. She stares so hard
at times she feels she might go blind. See one thing she has
to tell herself. See just one, small, thing. She almost can't do
it, and for a moment it seems as if her eyes will jut away and
out from her head altogether. And then a single palm-sized
object magnetizes her vision. Her breathing slows. Her shoulders let down. Her jaw and mouth slacken. Even her hair
calms, her head tilting slightly to the left. It is an indigo blue
earring dangling from the ear of a woman several rows up.
She cannot see it, but the woman has no arms.

Looking at the backs of people's heads too is a sort of brains-above-average jock guy. He's looking at the Seattle guy going, I bet that asshole has a goatee. I bet he smokes Dunhills. I bet his cigarette lighter is sterling silver. He's looking at the twitchy black and blue haired girl thinking this girl, she's gorgeous. Not in the conventional, anorexic, Gwyneth Paltrow way, the firm high barely there tits way, but in the I just got socked in the face and rolled in puddles on the bad side of town way. Like a bruise. If you ever saw *She's So Lovely* you know what he means by gorgeous. I'd bed her, he's going in his head, hell yeah. He's very close to becoming a Keanu, but he might get saved and become something more like a beefy stock broker. Of what Keanu has been saying he thinks, dude, I know what you mean. I read a book like that once too.

What I'm saying is you have to have some mental *gas* man, some stimuli, inspiration, some *juice* to drive you. You can't just stumble along into things without some inner resources (Here the Seattle guy is going, that's a fucking stolen line and I bet shit for brains doesn't even know it. That's a line from a poem. I confess, I have no inner resources. That's the fucking line. If he had any idea what he was talking about he'd know that the poet was making exactly the opposite point. This guy's like all surface…probably every experience he's ever had simply slides off of his skin like he's a linoleum table top. All sheen and glare (here the twitchy chick is thinking that is the most beautiful blue I have ever witnessed…it is so beautiful I think I might not be able to breathe, I think I might need medical attention. Her heart is racing faster than hummingbirds' wings, and her forehead feels tight (Here the jock thud-headed guy is thinking, yeah, like how I always keep a book of Bukowski around, you know, to take the edge off of things…it's better than drugs. That Bukowski man, he knew what was what.).).).

The actor stops speaking because the interviewer is engineering some more especially designed for Keanu Reeves questions. You know what I'm thinking, as I watch the way he sort of tilts his head to listen, and how he is gripping the arms of the chair in a kind of man way, and how his jaw occasionally looks strong, but from other angles slides into his neck (what's up with that?), and even how his eyes are almost black, I mean they must be dark brown, but they look black at times... I'm thinking that he wasn't so bad in *My Own Private Idaho*. I know, I can't believe I'm saying it either, but what I'm thinking is, in that role, there was this almost Shakespearian threshold which was both a limit to the character and a place of possibility. And that meant that his character could say truly idiotic things alongside truly profound things. And that was interesting. And he was good at it, and I think he was good at it because I get the sense that in real life he might be like that. He might say things once in a while which are mainline brilliant but have no idea at all what it is that he has said.

And another thing. That movie *The Matrix*. On the one hand, this is a movie almost tailor made for quintessential Keanu Reeves ridicule. No question. All that running around with his head cocked to the side like an over-aged child, all that "am I the one" crap looping the plot along exactly like the plot line of Jesus, and Keanu with a hole in his head...you can't beat that. On the other hand, there was this sort of beauty to the aestheticized violence which, one could argue, could ONLY have been achieved by one Mr. Keanu Reeves. And I say that because he's as aesthetically pleasing—and as equally empty—as a greek statue. So all of those slow-mo shots of him dodging bullets or twirling through the air in a weird stop action wrestle flight thing...it's like animating a Michelangelo, to a certain extent. Taking something static and making it dynamic. I mean think about it, if they had chosen a thinking man's actor, he could have never pulled it off. Can you picture Johnny Depp in that role? Or even, and I'm serious here, Brad Pitt? I think not. Maybe Tom Cruise....

Pretty much every other movie he ever made sucked ass. And I think you know what I mean.

It's like...it's like...(long pause. I mean a pause so long it looks directed) like an actor has to be three different beings. First, you have to be a guy who can absorb words and actions and through a kind of transformation, morph yourself into something you are not. Secondly, you have to take your thinking and release it—no, really, shoot it out over a landscape away from yourself like you are sending thought across some giant corn field in Iowa. I mean you have to let your brain go that far away from yourself or you can't let the art inhabit you. Thirdly, you have to live the art while you are doing it, you have to be that thing, which means you can't be whoever you are in your ordinary life. It might even mean you have no ordinary life, because there isn't space or time, especially if you are getting a lot of work, there's no room for you to be you since you have to be these other ...people. One hundred percent. So then what I'm saying is that acting alters being and knowing (Right this second the Seattle guy has something like a seizure, a flash, he is caught in a moment of almost pure understanding, like he's just comprehended Nietzsche perfectly and without exertion (Exactly at this moment the girl made of points starts, her eyes suck open and lock onto the actor, her breath catching in her throat, but wide and long and true, not hitching at all (Instantaneously the bulky nearly cognizant but not quite there for the thickness of his muscle matter thud head feels a slight tingle in his neck, which is actually a subtle rearranging of DNA, why, the boy may have a chance yet, it is entirely possible he will see something out of the corner of his eye which moves him toward thought, real thought,

thought which forces one through crucibles of struggle, thought without answer or ending, thought driving one to be a hunger artist, a perpetual explorer, aimed at nothing and everything, as wide as the white of a blank screen.).).). Yeah.

I have to admit, I like these "Actors Studio" interview thingees. Did you see the "Saturday Night Live" spoof on them? Funny as shit. As I am turning the television off to go write, I notice that next week is Brad Pitt. I hope he talks about working with Robert Redford. Now that would be a good show. I'd bring popcorn and beer for that one. An actor on an actor turned director and independent filmmaking saint. Fuck yeah.

I make my way to my desk. I've just now realized what I want the new screenplay to play out. It will feature a man whose conscious mind and subconscious mind are in reverse order. So that everything he thinks and says is as if he is using dreamspeak, as if he's crazy, as if he's not entirely here in the way that the rest of us are, but rather somewhere other, where language, image, and thought break back down into arbitrary parts. On the inside will be his order and logic, the distillation of chaos into patterns one can live with, the image by image splicing together of a life into a linear narrative one can understand.

Sometimes ideas just come like that.

Outtakes

FADE IN:

INT. 7-ELEVEN SOMEWHERE IN SOUTHERN CALIFORNIA.
1:00 AM

ANGLE ON:
The nametag of the clerk reads "Zeus." He's scratching his elbow; some kind of skin disease. His hair punked and bleached. Tongue stud. Tattoos sneaking out from the sleeves of his green uniform.

> ZEUS
> Yeah, I can see her as clear as day, man. She was a hottie. A real pocket rocker (laughing). Her lips, man. I never seen anything like 'em.

STOCK FOOTAGE of famous women from the nose down

> She had this little tattoo sneaking up her neck too, dude, it was some kind of snake or serpent shit or something.... What? Are you sure man? Fuck...well was she the one then who was kinda old, like thirty or some shit like that, the one with the spikey hair bleached

at the tips that kinda looked like Shania Twain
on acid? No? Fuck…well what'd she look like,
anyway?

INT. GOLD'S GYM SOMEWHERE IN SOUTHERN CALIFOR-
NIA

We see a punch to the face as if it has hit us dead on. Two
supermodels in Nike clothing and kick-boxing gear, one
stunned on the floor, one looking down at her. Black and
red Nike clothing. Red nails. Red lips. Both about a size
zero. One of the supermodels, the one on the floor, wears a
gold necklace in the shape of her name, "Kate." The other
has her name stitched on the ass of her Nike Lycra pants,
"Mew."

                  MEW
You O.K.?

                  KATE
Yeah. Swell.

KATE gets up off of the floor, shakes her head some.

                  MEW
Cool.

                  KATE
Actually she trained with us for about six
months. Wasn't it?

                  MEW
Yeah. I think so.

                         KATE

We all had the same trainer. Sensei Marc.

                         MEW

He had the idea that we train together. Three-
some.

STOCK FOOTAGE of *Charlie's Angels*

                         KATE

Perv.

                         MEW

Fucker.

                         KATE

Anyway. We got good enough to spar. All of
us. And instead of sparring with people in
the other classes, we sparred with each other.
To practice.

                         MEW

She was definitely the best of the three of us.
She nailed me in the head once so precisely
my ears rang for about a month. I think my
equilibrium was off for a while too; I kept
misjudging doorways and table corners, almost falling when I got up out of chairs.

                         KATE

Yeah, I remember that…it was a spinning
knife kick, wasn't it? You'd be surprised how
high we can kick with these legs.

MEW

What do you want to know?

KATE

Definitely. She could have taken a guy... particularly if he wasn't expecting it. Like some fat ass bank guard, no problem. Or a security guy off his doughnut break. Yeah, I think she could have stunned or even taken a guy out.

MEW

Or she could have dosed him with a series of blows, then kicked the shit out of him. I mean, some of these moves can be *lethal*, you understand? This isn't aerobics. You'd be surprised.

KATE

So did she? Did she take a guy out? I mean, I'm just curious. I just want to know. Did she do any damage? Because if she did, I mean, I'd just *really* want to know about it. I always thought she could take someone out. The first thing anyone ever noticed about her was those lips. Drop dead gorgeous. But she could drop you dead for real. I guess I'd just once like to see that. You know? So, what, did she?

INT. 7-ELEVEN SOMEWHERE IN SOUTHERN CALIFORNIA. 1:00 AM.

ANGLE ON:

ZEUS still trying to remember. Helping a customer or two, having trouble giving them correct change since he is stoned.

ZEUS

Wait. Dude, was she the one with the nasty
blonde dreads and that pierced shit on her
face? Oh man. Cuz if it was her then, shit
yeah, I got a story to tell. She was one crazy
bitch. There was this one time, I'm pretty sure
she was methed out...she had that hyper
twitch speed thing going on, and she came
in with this other chick, some Asian hottie,
and it was REAL near closing time. They
brought all this beer and shit up to the counter
and she says, get this man, she says, uh, we
don't have any ACTUAL money (stoner
laugh). And I say, well, I don't have any
ACTUAL beer to sell you. But hey, I could
maybe DONATE this VIRTUAL beer to you
two, because, I mean, dude, they were both
HOTTIES, man, their tits alone could have lit
that fucking 7-Eleven neon sign up...what?

We see SLOW MOTION action of the tits of two women.

ZEUS
Oh. Sorry, man. Then which one was she?

INT. PSYCHIATRIST OFFICE. NIGHT

The gold and fake wood thing on the desk reads "Dr. Freed."
There are more books in the office than probably anyone
has read, arranged stylishly on bookshelves from Pottery
Barn. All the furniture in the office is from Pottery Barn—
black leather mostly. Clever area rugs. Silver and black framed
photographs peppering the room. His diplomas and cre-
dentials are also arranged in an almost excruciatingly

aesthetically pleasing way on the walls. He is of course smoking a cigar; the smoke curls around his mouth and face just like in a movie. SLOW MOTION.

>   DR. FREED
> You understand of course that I cannot divulge any actual information about our relationship, either implicit or explicit...you understand that I am bound to a set of ethical codes with regard to her as a patient?

ANGLE ON:

DR. FREED watching the interviewer take her seat, unable to take his eyes away, standing for a moment directly in front of the couch, his crotch staged at eye level, his hand resting briefly at his hip.

>   DR. FREED
> What I can do, however, in an effort to help you, is narrate the surrounding information, or add to the information you have already presented me with, in a kind of "roman à clef." Do you see? Particularly if she is in some kind of danger, or, perish the thought, worse.... I often thought that her tremendously sexual presence would draw...well, you know the world we live in. You are a beautiful woman, you must understand your environment, the world of men, of sexual predation, with a certain complexity.

STOCK FOOTAGE of rape threat scenarios

DR. FREED

What? Yes. I am well aware that she was a black belt.

STOCK FOOTAGE of men being emasculated

DR. FREED

Let's get on with things. What was it you were saying earlier? If I am not mistaken, you said something about her bisexual tendencies. You wanted a professional rather than secular account. I admire your efforts. Most people are only interested in tabloid renditions of reality these days. Bad B-movies.

There is a way in which bisexuality, theoretically at least, saves the Oedipus complex from simple gender determinism, yes? We've come a long way in the last century. In our better understanding we see that bisexuality shifts its meaning and comes to stand for the very uncertainty of sexual division itself. It is, if you will, an in between zone, a place between choices. Once the patient resolves this uncertainty, either as a heterosexual or as a homosexual, for we of course no longer treat homosexuality as a disease, as a condition to heal oneself from, they can almost always achieve a full and happy relationship, complete with commitment.

DR. FREED strokes his beard and licks his lips.

DR. FREED

As with you, it was the case with her that a

young woman so beautiful...that is, it would
be a shame to lose her.

DR. FREED smiles while stroking his beard. He almost winks.

DR. FREED
What? Good lord. I'm merely attempting to
answer your questions. You asked me about
her inclinations, her sexual predispositions.
That IS why she came. To see me. Her un-
conscious desires were making a mess of her
life, and she wanted to resolve things, one
way or another, as I stated. You see, today
we understand bisexuality in quite sophisti-
cated ways. It can be said to be either a theo-
retical wish, or a socialization practice, more
crassly put I suppose as a trendy stopgap for
the young, akin to grunge music or the modern primitive impulses of tattooing and pierc-
ing. You see it everywhere; it is a fashion.
But more seriously for some, it is the ob-
stacle in the way of normal and long lasting
human relationships. This "either/or" condition. This wavering between things.

DR. FREED waves his hand back and forth in the air, then
makes a little fist with it.

DR. FREED
She came because she was lodged so tightly
in an in-between world as to almost be para-
lytic. Do you see? A beautiful young woman
in the prime of her life. But the literal reason
was that she was having stalker fantasies.

CLIPS from STOCK FOOTAGE of famous stalkers

DR. FREED

Hmm? No. She was not being stalked. She
was having fantasies of stalking someone.

But it really begins before that. Inside of a
deeper story. You see, she had an obsession.
No. That is incorrect. She had a complex fixa-
tion based on the obsessions of her dead
brother; she was thus obsessed with the obsessions of a dead man obsessed with another dead man. I see already that you are
perplexed. Let me narrate. It seems that her
brother, with whom she may have been in
love, but certainly to whom she developed
an obsession after his untimely death in a car
accident, her brother was obsessed with
James Dean—this you know.

DR. FREED licks his lips.

As you may or may not know, Dean was a
bisexual. Though he preferred to be referred
to as an "explorer," in this as in all his adven-
tures, and of course biographers and busy-
bodies debate this business as a marketing
ploy. But what is important here is that Jimmy,
her brother, identified with Dean both as a
young man in the midst of authority battles
and as a startlingly beautiful man attracted to
both men and to women. On the face of it
one might not think this makes much of a
difference; however, if you go back and
study the film *Rebel Without a Cause,* if you,

in effect, "re-read" the scenes that might be relevant to a man obsessed with Dean as a love object and second self, well, I think you would agree with me that the movie takes on a myriad of possible meanings. For instance, the scenes between Jim and Plato.

James Dean FILM FOOTAGE

Yes? And once you have understood that relationship, you would then need to probe deeper, for L.'s love for her brother was predicated on his love for Dean; therefore, what L. loved was not Dean's representation, but the representation of a representation. And what she wanted more than to have her brother, who of course wished to be Dean, was to *be* her brother wishing to be Dean. Are you getting the picture?

Oh, he enacted a whole list of small time crimes, probably inspired by the movie of course. Petty theft, stolen cars, a feeble attempt at a bank robbery. They were a bit like parodies of a delinquency that no longer has currency. He raced cars, too, I mean after hours with friends for money and testosterone highs, no doubt. And in the end, he died in a kind of aestheticized repeat of Dean's famous car wreck. Same car, only the whole accident was constructed, almost staged. You know, money can buy you anything these days, even your own death, even a story of your death.

What? Yes. She was not your average client from the get-go. There was a point in time where I began to be concerned about her in a professional sense. Her tales about her brother, combined with her narrations about her inability to center herself in her own present life, and perhaps most importantly her fantasies about stalking a man—an actor it is reported to be true has been signed to perform in the film biography of Dean—*as well as* stalking a woman—the girlfriend of her dead brother—left me wondering if perhaps this beautiful and clearly brilliant girl had perhaps a more disturbing disorder than I originally thought. It wasn't so much the fantasies themselves, but rather the stories of action she narrated...they were positively dreamy, as seductive as any roman à clef. Why, I remember watching her leave the office on occasion after one of these stories with the distinct feeling that a deep seduction had occurred, one from which I might not be able to break the spell.

DR. FREED is looking off into space, almost dreamily. The smoke from his cigar is perfectly suspended in the air. He has the look of pleasure on his face.

DR. FREED

What? Good lord no. What has caused you to ask such an insulting question? Ridiculous. I did see her after the abrupt termination of her visits. At the market, where she appeared to be in some kind of trance or daze over the meat; another time I saw her very late at night

in the park near her apartment. She was sitting on a bench talking to herself. And there
was the time I saw her downtown; she took
a cab to a popular alternative bar, then another to an Indian restaurant where she
dined alone. The third cab she took that
night went into an area of the city where I
have heard after hours clubs host all kinds
of troubled people. What? What are you
suggesting? Look I don't have to talk to you.
Look you have misinterpreted what I have
said. You come in here, you tell me on what
now appear to be false pretenses that the
girl is missing, possibly dead, you come in
here dressed like that.... What? How dare
you. Get out of here. This "interview" is of-
ficially over. You are very rude. Have you
no integrity? This is an ethical issue. You
have no idea. Get out.

INT. 7-ELEVEN. 1:00 AM

ZEUS shooting spit wads at the ceiling. Pausing for an instant as if he has had an epiphany.

                    ZEUS
Oh shit man, what are those things called
when you remember something? You know ·
when you get that kind of bolt of lightning in
between the eyes shit? Yeah dude, epiphany.
I'm having one of them. Dude. She had big
lips, right? And her eyes kinda had that glazed-
over look like she was on Dilaudin, correct?
Eh? Am I right? I got her, baby. I got her fixed

in my mind's eye now. All right now. You're gonna love this shit.

                                    CUT TO:

JEM walking into a 7-Eleven where ZEUS is working.

                    ZEUS
Aren't you kinda late, man?

                    JEM
Zeus, baby, you might want to ease up on the visual aids. I'm an hour early.

                    ZEUS
Oh, right, shit yeah. O.K. Dang, woman, you look all hot and shit.

                    JEM
Calm down before you rupture something.

                    ZEUS
So you ready?

                    JEM
Yes, Zeus. Maybe we should talk about it like this for a while first so the cameras get the whole thing on film. Huh?

                    ZEUS
What?

                    JEM
Nevermind.

ZEUS
Oh, shit…that's a joke, right? DUDE. I get it.

JEM
You know, Zeus, sometimes you look just
like Jiminy Cricket.

ZEUS
You mean that little insect dude with the top
hat and cane?

JEM
That's right, brainiac.

ZEUS
Kinda Hanna-Barbera you mean.

JEM
No, kinda little cartoon cricket with oversized
head singing a surrealistic song.

ZEUS pauses not knowing whether or not to laugh. JEM and
ZEUS stare at each other.

JEM
Are you looking at my tits, Zeus?

ZEUS
No, man, jesus…

We see a CLOSE UP of JEM's tits.

STOCK FOOTAGE of women's tits

                              JEM
          Let's do it.

                              ZEUS
          Fuck yeah.

JEM quickly pulls a 9mm 92FS Beretta from her inside coat
pocket and points it at ZEUS's face.

                              JEM
          Give me everything you got or I'll blow that
          fucking dumbass grin right off of your
          goddamn face.

                              ZEUS
          I don't want any trouble, lady.

ZEUS begins to give her the money he has access to in a
kind of exaggerated cartoon way. JEM stuffs it into a paper
bag.

                              JEM
          Stop grinning, Zeus. You look like an idiot.

                              ZEUS
          Yes Ma'am!!

JEM takes the bag and walks out of the store. ZEUS watches
her, mutters "thank you for shopping" underneath his breath,
then calls the police.

                              ZEUS
          Then we'd meet back up at my place around
          3 AM and fuck like bunnies.

CUT TO:

ZEUS's ratty-ass little studio apartment where he and a woman whose face you can't see burst in kissing and groping each other. Then the SHOT FREEZES.

ZEUS

No, wait, man. That wasn't her. I mean about the bunny fucking. But we did get it on, in my car. Always in my car.

CUT TO:

ZEUS's beater-mobile of a car in an abandoned parking lot. All kinds of shit litters the inside of the car...old 7-Eleven bags and plastic cups, Jack-in-the-Box stuff, etc.... ZEUS is in the front seat and a woman whose face we can't see is riding him for all she is worth. ZEUS moves to grab her tits. Then the SHOT FREEZES.

ZEUS

Oh fuck. Maybe we got it on in the bath-room of Denny's.... Or was that that other chick with one leg shorter than the other?

ZEUS appears lost in thought in 7-Eleven.

ZEUS

Anyway, things went like that. What? Once a month. For about four months. Practice runs. Dude, I almost got fired even. Well, she made herself look different every time. One time she even did it as a man. No, dude, I'm seri-ous. And every month like clockwork I got

my cut underneath my car—strapped to the
axle. Killer, huh?

INT. CALIFORNIA PRISON

A television in a day room with the movie *Rebel Without a
Cause* on. The names of men who have visitors can be heard
over a loudspeaker. Men raise their hands one at a time.
When the name "Buzz Stark" is called, a man separates himself from the crowd of orange-suited men, steps forward.
He has a scar across his right eye. He is handsome in an old
movie star way. He is smoking a Camel cigarette and his
walk looks almost rehearsed. He walks over to a table and
sits down.

> BUZZ
> I don't know why I should talk to you. I don't
> even know you. I don't care about you. Like,
> at all. Why should I talk to you?

BUZZ looks up at the television for a while. Then back to
the interviewer.

> BUZZ
> What do I get out of this deal? I'll tell you
> what. Jack shit. Look at you. With your little
> tape recorder. You look jack-asstic is how.
> Fucking cunt. Who do you think you are? I
> don't have to tell you diddly. What?

BUZZ looks right and then left.

> BUZZ
> Are you telling me you're holding?

BUZZ reaches a hand underneath the table. He stares straight ahead. The interviewer jerks away, and he pulls his hand back up.

                    BUZZ
You come prepared. Maybe there is something I can tell you. She had a sweet pussy. She had the sweetest pussy I ever saw. And her tits. Man. Like perfect champagne glasses. Her nipples round and hard in your mouth. Look, if you wanted the G-rated version you shouldn't have come here. I mean, look around you. Cuz every guy here is looking at you the same way. You are the SHOW, baby. We're the audience.

No, man, I met her by accident. Her brother used to be my outside connection. Then he suicided or something and BANG, she just shows up to visit one day. It was kinda eerie, I have to admit, because I knew who she was the second I laid eyes on her.

                                    CUT TO:

Inside a California prison visiting area. JEM is picking a scab on her arm. BUZZ walks up and sits down.

                    BUZZ
Well, what the fuck do we have here?

                    JEM
Nothing to get excited about. Sit down.

BUZZ

You Jem? You Jimmy's little piece of tail sister? Well I'll be a goddamned son of a bitch.
What are you doing here, girl? You got no
place here.

JEM

I got a place here. I got the same place my
brother had. You still need someone on the
outside, right?

BUZZ stares at JEM, smiling.

JEM

I'm your man.

BUZZ

You're no man, tits.

BUZZ leans over very close to JEM, close enough so that the
stubble on his face is magnified to cinematic proportions.

BUZZ

Listen here, tits. You don't know how things
go down in this line of work. You can't just
waltz in here and act like you own the place.
So you can just turn around and take that
little pink ass out of here.

BUZZ gets up to leave, laughing under his breath.

JEM

I got a twat full of something that says I do
know how things work. You gonna pass up
the chance to feel me up?

BUZZ stops. Turns around. Comes back. Reaches underneath the table between them until his hands are making
their way up JEM's skirt. JEM spreads her legs.

                        BUZZ
        Talk to me, tits. You gotta talk or they'll hassle
        me. Come on now, little sister, that's right.
        Just open up.

                        JEM
        Your mamma says to write her more. She's
        sick. She's got the flu. She's got a fever.

BUZZ manages to get a plastic bag filled with dope ex-
tracted from between JEM's legs. He smiles.

                        BUZZ
        That's good, sister, real good. Now what do
        you want? Cuz I know it ain't my birthday.
        What's the dope?

                        JEM
        Information. I want you to tell me step by
        step how to make an explosive device seri-
        ous enough to take out a building the size of
        a movie theater.

                        BUZZ
        You want to blow up a movie theater?

                        JEM
        No, brainiac. That's just the size of the build-
        ing.

BUZZ

What, a bank? And just what does little miss
twinkle twat think she's gonna do then?

JEM

It's not a bank, and it's none of your fucking
business. And that's not all.

BUZZ (V.O.)

Then she takes out this list, and on the list
are five crimes. Crimes she says are the most
popular in the eyes of society. The most popular. She's got car theft, robbery, drug smug-
gling, murder, and bombing on the list. She
tells me she wants a shot-to-shot script of
how to accomplish each.

JEM

Look. I got what you need. I got what my
brother had and more. I'll be here once a
week, with dope every time. I believe that
keeps you where you want to be. You edu-
cate me and I give you what you want.

BUZZ stares at her for a long minute and then starts to get
up and leave.

JEM

Baby, don't go yet. I got something else for
you.

BUZZ

What's that?

BUZZ sits back down, laughing. JEM grabs his crotch underneath the table. She unzips his pants. She takes his dick out, gives him a hand job. Eventually he closes his eyes.

> JEM
>
> I'm gonna talk to you so nobody harasses you. Think about these lips wrapped around your cock. Oh yeah. Think about sliding your dick down my throat some, giving me a pearl of come. I can taste you. Can you feel me tasting you, baby?

> BUZZ
>
> Oh yeah baby sister…give it to me….

JEM stops.

> BUZZ
>
> No baby, you don't stop now, give ol' Buzz the works…. Think of it as a first installment….

BUZZ grabs her hand and tries to return it to his crotch. JEM jerks it away.

> BUZZ
>
> What the fuck? You some kinda prick tease?

> JEM
>
> I'll be back next week…what, don't you get it, Buzz? We were just playing chicken. I just had to prove my manhood.

CUT TO:

Present interview in prison.

BUZZ

So that's how we met. And that's how things
went down for about three months. Every
time she came in she looked different too;
once I almost didn't recognize her. But it
turned me on, I mean it kept things interesting. It was like a new *Playboy* calendar pin-
up coming every week. Why? Because it felt
good. No. Not just getting each other off. It
was more than that. It's like she understood
something about a man. Once she took a
photo of me. She brought it to me...black
and white. In the picture I was laughing. I've
never seen myself laugh. You don't understand what it is to never have anything but
shit reflected back to you. Every damn day
of your life. Every man likes to feel like they
are worth something. Like they are good at
something. Like somebody gives a fuck. She
was a good woman. Inside and out...and she
kicked ass on her brother, no doubt. Yeah?
Well, if what you are telling me is true, then
I was a good goddamn teacher, wasn't I? They
oughta fucking give me a diploma or something. Yeah? Then they oughta give her an
Academy Award. Fuck yeah.

INT. BAR IN L.A. NIGHT

From floor level we see the feet of regular patrons in the
bar. Cowboy boots, old worn-out shoes, work boots, shoes
of all sorts. Underneath one particular table we visually climb
a pair of white go-go boots. At the knee we shift to a view of
hands on the table. Large fake gems decorate the fingers of

a woman who is very clearly about 80 years old. Up her arms are bangles. Her hair is dyed red. Her chin juts out since she is holding her head high. She has the look of a kind of sassy, classy rodent; small features and quick eyes. Behind her head is a sign on the wall of the bar that reads: "If you need to know my name you came to the wrong woman." She is drinking scotch on the rocks and sizing up the interviewer.

> WOMAN
>
> There's something about you. No, I'm saying, I can't quite put my finger on it, but it will come to me. Don't say anything. Let me just look at you for a minute. I said don't say anything for chrissakes. I'm using some of what you call women's intuition. Don't interrupt me.

The WOMAN closes her eyes.

> WOMAN
>
> You ever been to Del Mar? To the tracks? You ever do the ponies?

The WOMAN opens one of her eyes.

> WOMAN
>
> No? Well, it'll come to me. Just talk to me for a while. Eventually it'll pop up just like a strudel.

The WOMAN claps her hands together and laughs.

> WOMAN
>
> A person could say I was the only eyewitness to the accident. No, really. While the

rest of the beach-world was doing that kind
of late summer swelling into fall thing, you
know, the smell of coconut oil and beer fading to bonfires and wool blankets, I had my
metal detector out, my earphones on, my
mind as clear and wide as the ocean.

Southern California beach scene, ANGLE ON an old woman
in a kind of muumuu wearing metal detector gear, a broad
straw hat, and stylish sunglasses panning the sand.

> WOMAN (V.O.)
> I like to close my eyes when I'm hunting for
> metal. Let my intuition lead me, let my con-
> scious mind slip back, my subconscious lean
> forward. You know what I'm saying. That day
> I'd already scored what appeared to be a
> working Rolex, quite a find, really, and some
> change, and then I hit on a larger object,
> which is always a little exciting, you under-
> stand.

The WOMAN looks as if she is zapped with electricity; she
stops in her tracks and toes the sand with one foot.

> WOMAN (V.O.)
> I'm not saying I saw the thing itself, mind
> you. I'm not saying I saw it shot-to-shot or
> anything like that. Why, it was up the bluff
> from where I was hunting metal for one thing,
> and the sun was high enough in the sky to
> blind anyone looking up.

Image of the ocean. The sand. The blue of the sky. Little
glittery things in the sand.

WOMAN (V.O.)

What I'm saying is that I found scraps of metal like breadcrumbs leading from me, down on the shore, to her, up the bluff. One at a time. After about the third object, part of a side mirror, I realized what was what. Objects just don't fall from the sky in patterns, like, that is what I'm saying.

Image of a side mirror falling from the sky in SLOW MO-TION, landing in the sand.

WOMAN (V.O.)

I'm going to be honest with you. The first thing I thought was that I was going to find a body. A young, male, beautiful body. Because the beach is filled with young beautiful males all summer, like some neverending movie. No, really, it's like a constant supply of gum-drops or pennies from heaven. They're just luscious.

Images of beautiful boys on the beach—playing frisbee, car-rying surfboards, scoping chicks.

WOMAN (V.O.)

And you know they're all on dope and dreamy and moving through their youth like shooting marbles. So what I thought I was going to find was one of those beauties wrapped directly around a telephone pole or something. Going 80, 90, 100 miles an hour around that bluff in Daddy's car, Ray Bans and shirtless and hair blowing like a maga-zine advertisement. Dashful of pills, some

girl's panties in the back seat. When you do
what I do for as many years as I have the
whole world sets up like little pieces you can
track and collect.

Image of the WOMAN finding metal objects from a car one
at a time.

CUT TO:

Back in the dimly lit bar, the WOMAN swirling ice around in
her glass, drinking, holding the liquor in her mouth a few
seconds before closing her eyes and swallowing.

WOMAN
A lot of the people that live in SoCal are role
playing. The whole area is like a veneer or
Hollywood set, and people sort of move
around artificial-like, like they are trying to
fit a story of themselves. I'm not sure when it
happened exactly, but once it did it was as if
the whole population had been strangely
anesthetized or knocked out. Out there.

The WOMAN gestures toward the door with her glass.

WOMAN
Alls you have to do is listen, watch. What
you'll see is people acting like people...no, I
mean *acting*. Everything out of their mouths
sounds scripted and flat, like you could push
a rewind button at any moment, or change
the hair on the blonde to red with a few clicks
of a button.

STOCK FOOTAGE of Southern California babes in rapid
succession

The WOMAN leans in closer to the interviewer.

> WOMAN
>
> Wrecks on that particular turn were frequent;
> well, not frequent in terms of the way you
> young people experience things. But frequent
> when the definition meant something. I mean,
> since I've been here there have been maybe
> ten crashes, each more glorious than the next,
> almost always young, beautiful men, drunk,
> high, or depressed. But the way things hap-
> pen now.... I mean, speed's the main thing
> now. There are ten stories of violence a night
> on the nightly news, so one car wreck can
> hardly carry weight, now can it?

We see a talking news head on the television above the
bartender's head. The images are of some random car wreck.

> CUT TO:

Smoke just visible over the crest of a hill in the road. People
in nearby apartments poking their heads out of their doors,
looking at each other and in the direction of the smoke.

> WOMAN (V.O.)
>
> One thing that pissed me off, I mean it really
> got my panties in a wad, was that people
> around here started claiming to know her after
> I found her. And so when the television trucks
> stationed themselves outside our apartments
> everybody who was usually inside hiding like

moles came out to shoot their mouth off, to blab out some fiction that made them feel important, hoping for a "spot." Christ. This is the world we live in.

CUT TO:

Bar scene.

> WOMAN
>
> I mean, don't you find it repugnant how people claim ownership of violence after the fact? Forget slowing down to do the peeping tom number on a car crash, now people want in on the action. They want to say they knew her therapist. Her lover. They want to say she was working on a movie, that they had her car done at their garage, that they saw her with someone mysterious looking at some chichi-ass restaurant. I mean what I'm saying is they wanted her to be someone famous so that they could talk about knowing someone famous.

We see the image of a famous person selling something in a commercial on the bar's television.

> WOMAN
>
> Pieces of human excrement. That's what I'm saying. Because not one of them knew her. Not one of them saw the wreck. Not one of them was there when I found her crumpled like a wadded up piece of paper in her car, her boot toes setting off my detector like a siren.

Image of feet and the sound of a metal detector going nuts.

WOMAN (V.O.)

But what I was thinking as I was making my
way up the bluff was that one of these little
greek gods had gone and fucked up. And I
was thinking how all those little greek god
deaths sort of repeated and accumulated.
How they stood for something that maybe
was the other side of the teen idol.... Look,
you can't live in Southern California without
understanding that the central symbol for life
down here is the movie star...maybe for everyone everywhere. Only, in little pockets or
on the sides of actual roads they're lining up
like road kill. Always have. I don't mean in a
big huge cinematic tragic way. I mean in an
ordinary way.

I remember my live-in beau at the time was
a retired smack addict—horny old bastard I'll
tell you what—I don't know if that Viagra is
a blessing or a curse—anyway. We were
watching videos one night, and I turned to
him and said Wayne, you know what I think?
I said I think it all boils down to those
goddamn Greeks. And Wayne said, what the
hell are you talking about? So I turned the
sound down for a minute and said the
Greeks—the way they made out like the
young naked boy was the height of art. The
purest form of beauty. I think we've been
stuck on that feed for a long time. But nobody wants to admit it. And Wayne said, get
out of here. Nothing is more prevalent in

popular culture than tits and ass and blondes. And that ain't Greek. That's American.

I had to admit he had a point. But then I pointed out how all the popular movies had these male leads that were either very young, or very virile even if they weren't young (you got your Mel Gibsons and your Kevin Costners, for chrissakes. God help us). And I added that the tits and ass are only there so that more young men will go see movies about themselves. And think of all the popular movies with no women in them at all, Wayne, like sometimes what the men are doing is so fucking fantastic you don't even need women at all. I was thinking of old movies, new movies, and everything in between. I mean, I can name 'em, can't you? I know that you can. Wayne went silent at this and so I turned the sound back up. I think we were watching *Apocalypse Now*. Or maybe it was *The Usual Suspects, Butch Cassidy and the Sundance Kid, Cool Hand Luke,* or *Good-Fellas.*

So when I walked up that bluff and located the car and came around to the driver's side and my detector went berserk and I saw blonde hair undulating with the wind, I was a little stunned. I mean I stopped in my tracks a bit. And the first clear thought I had upon seeing her was my god, what an oddly beautiful image, since she was smiling, I kid you not. And I can't be sure of this, but I think her eyes were open. And the second thing I

thought was jesus christ, that's a Porsche
Spyder, isn't that the car James Dean died in?
And the third thing I thought before I could
stop myself was, aren't they making a movie
about his life, and wasn't Brad Pitt up for the
part?

Of course then I snap to and run like a ban-
shee back down the bluff to a phone and I
call the police and get my ass back up that
goddamn bluff but you know what? There's
no woman in the car anymore. She's out of
the picture entirely. But on the car seat is a
pile of silver jewelry, quarters, dimes, a com-
pact mirror, a little tin box filled with pot,
and enough metal to let me take a few days
off and sit by the pool drinking Mai-Tai's with
my feet propped up.

You think she's out there? You think she just
got up and walked away? Because I don't
mind telling you, that's one woman I'd like
to meet. See these boots? I bought 'em the
very next day. Let's drink to that. Let's you
and me drink to that. You know, I kind of
like you. There's something about you. There
just is.

Blue Movie

One.

> Your *no* has driven me from your house, your street,
> whole cities; a mouth driving me out of a country,
> skyward. This flight. To everyone else you speak
> playful flutters of words in the color of amber.
> People's eyes follow your words as if golden and
> red hewn butterflies swim around their heads. You
> do this. I've watched you. To me, underneath the
> cover of words, there lies only one.

Two.

> In this city which is not you, not your name, not
> the deep red of your unspeakable hair, I am nam-
> ing you. I know what you want is *les cartes postales.*
> I know what you want is words from me scrawled
> on white, their enigmatic beauty graphic and inde-
> cipherable to you: *il n'a pas de quoi.* But in this city
> which is not you I am moving, lunging, anything
> instead of naming you. *Je ne t'appelle pas.* I am not
> naming in every object, in people's faces or ges-
> tures. In glasses of wine. In drunk walks along the
> river. In passing out on the floor, once, on cement,
> under a bridge. In the blue silk scarf I bought for
> you and wear myself: wave of night. In men along
> the river, my skirt lifted easily as dark falling, in the

smell of urine in an alley, in a cognac and jazz at an hour not night nor day. In the bee keeper selling me honey, in the plums I put in my mouth, in café windows and museum corridors and underneath the city, the metro's labyrinths. Mornings too, this city kissed by sun, her cathedral towers like hedonistic tits rising up to the mouth of a sky. A river running like blood in a vein, and this too, is you, my veins aching, my mouth watering. In books smelling of mildew and paper and history. I have unnamed you hundreds of times. Your name in my mouth is more than language itself. It is easy; you are as absent of meaning as an abstract color in a foreign language. *Rouge. Mon Dieu.*

Three.

Tu es un photo qui dormir.

Forgive me. I beg you to forgive my surrender to you. I have had something like a vision in which you figure more prominently than my own blood. You know, blood is not red. It is a tromp l'oeil. It is instead blue, like veins. We only perceive it as red when oxygen, life-giver, meets it. I do not mean to frighten you with talk like that. I know about ordinary relationships, about patience, fear of going under. You have explained it to me hundreds of times. Or else you have not explained it at all, you have said absolutely nothing, *rien,* and I was listening more intently than I have ever listened in my life. But what I am is so far beyond that ordinary set of structures it is almost laughable. Either you will listen or you will not. If I speak things aloud more than likely you will not listen. If I write them there is at least a chance that you will read them. You have always been this way. It matters little, can you see? If you take these words in, my life has meaning. If you do not, I am at the cusp I have always been at, ready to give in at the slightest brush of wind.

This digression is irritating. I would consume my own fingers if I thought I could lose you by misspeaking. What's happened is this. I have begun to picture you. But more; beyond the ordinary machinations of the mind, the regular fantasizing about a figure, first static, then perhaps through desire in some "scene," I have moved far beyond that. My image of you is as a waking dream, lucid, complex, mobile. You have invaded my very life. I see you walk into a café where I am having coffee and reading the newspaper. Do not misread me here. I don't "imagine" that I see you, I do. You are present, you come through the door, you walk toward me, you take your seat, and your stare is unflinching. The first time it happened I thought I might need medical attention.

The second time it happened I was in a bar, a darkly lit place much comforting and anonymous, I was drinking scotch and again you entered, you broke through the dark with a walking that brought every hair on my body to stand on end, again you came to me, and to no one else in the room, as a movie broke loose from the screen, as theater let loose from psychology and action.

And I did not hesitate to reach out to you, to touch you, and I can only imagine how I appeared to the other patrons of the place or to anyone watching, gesturing to nothing, I don't know, how can I know what is seen in this world?

Every night that I do not have this experience, by
this I mean every night that you do not move from
the film of my mind to the experience of my body, I
am tortured, I am near an unbearable longing ripping flesh and cracking bone, I want to tear my own
eyes out or hair or I don't know what. I do what you
do, but for different reasons entirely. I mimic you
out of order. I go to films to relieve the explosive
ache; the dark, the women larger than life, desire set
forth into huge colors and movement. You are therefore blond. Like me. I have given you my hair.
Forgive me.

Four.

I have stared at my own hand until the mound of
your shoulder touched the cup of my palm. I have
closed my eyes and pressed my face between folds
of flesh, in the places where skin meeting skin sends
convulsion and quiver. I have forgotten my name in
between your breasts, breathing in the sweet warm,
nuzzling the unbearably soft swells. In the under-
belly of your abdomen I have brushed my cheek
like a child, in the dip of your back I have been
cradled. And when this world I see brought your
gesture through the distance between us and on me,
I sank to the floor, I poured like liquid into the puddle
of body made of your touch on my flesh. I have
written this phrase over and over and over again
only so that I may live here, with you, in you, without end: *elle ne me touche pas; elle est l'image vîte.*

I know not to tell you this. I know the danger. I had
not intended to write this, but how can I put something down which does not say how your tenderness sleeps in the tips of my fingers, how your breath

pushes each of my lungs open and closed, how the features of your face have been traced with my tongue in the morning, when you broke from sleep, covered with dew, rose and sand colored glorious?

Perhaps it is simple. Perhaps I am a victim of my age, this age. I have seen too many movies with women in them that undo me. Let's talk about Duras. Or Winterson. I've always wanted to speak with you about Kim Novak, particularly in the movie *Vertigo*. Let's have a conversation, let's talk about books and movies. No. Perhaps things are even more stark and pathetic than that; perhaps I have had too much to drink. Scotch, the finest. My socks never match. My heart leaded in my chest. My jaw too big, isn't it? We'd laugh if you were here.
Forgive me.
Yours.

Five.

Years have been less torture than minutes. I know how overdramatic I sound, honestly. It's ludicrous. It's unanswered. You do not come, will never. Still. I picture you in scenes of longing so great my brain nearly explodes inside the shell of its skull. I picture you framed in a great cinematic square open to thousands of voyeuristic eyes eating at you from the distance of a theater. I picture you with almost no notion of humanity, or else with such humanity that it dissolves the image as if by fire.

Because of the blue beads I bought and placed inside a wooden box a hundred years old; because of the indigo china plate on which I place food for every meal that I eat; because of my eyes in the

mirror; because of the water reflecting the sky outside of my apartment; because of the way the light
catches the veins of my arm, or those near my eye
(I am older than you, the traces of time moving
like tiny rivers underneath the surface of my skin);
because of the silk I buy for you, send to you, my
hands lost in it before it crosses oceans; because
of the cornflowers I fill the rooms with; because
of a necklace I have purchased for you but am
unable to remove from my own neck; because of
the dress of a little girl at the river's edge in a
movie; because of all this, this scene has been
above all tortuous:

You are in a blue room. Blue walls. Blue floors. Blue
tables, blue ceiling, blue in darks and lights. There is
scotch being served; a few other people are in the
room, two couples, a man by himself, a woman at a
bar. There is a male bartender and one other man
behind the bar smoking a cigar. You are on a blue
sofa against a wall.

The camera pans the room painfully slowly. It finally, when the viewer feels as if they might strike
someone from waiting, lands on you. Your face is
larger than the frame; you bleed beyond vision. Your
lips are blue. Your eyelids are blue. Your mouth
shows indigo from in between barely parted lips.
Your hair is translucent blue. Your neck, blue. Your
dress scoops down to your breasts, rising and falling, sky, heaves of sky.

In the film it is clear from plot that one of the men in
the room has had you and his want lingers like blue
smoke. In the film it is also indicated that one of the

women wants you and her desire is submerged in waves of water as sound disappears into echo.

You rise from your sitting and your body engulfs the entire room to blue. Only Marguerite Duras has ever written a scene such as the one you inhabit. Only Kim Novak ever had a body as huge as the body that takes that room to blue to black, bruised incomprehensible. Kim Novak; you know her? I know that you know her. I am certain of this even if it is untrue.

When the camera fades to black you are taking off your dress while at the same time you are lighting a match and setting your own blue-blond hair on fire. Men and women burn from the body, your mouth is huge and laughing, your eyes are murderously open, your head is thrown back in delight.

The room is consumed by blue. I do not know how to return. I do not know how to come to you. You did not come. Won't ever. Your *no* in your mouth pooling like azure.

This distance all of language, wide as a cinema scene. This sentence. This page. Yours.

Shooting

She pulls up to a stop sign like blood throb. Says, motherfucker. She can feel like a bruised shoulder that she has a flat. She can feel like a leaded left arm that she has a flat. She can feel front left. She wheels it over to the curb. Crippled like that. Her jaw aches. Her left eye twitches.

Fucking jack. Fucking spare. Fucking tire iron. Truncated lines stack themselves in her skull like that. The line "ten years." The line "suffering makes us stronger." She sets up the metal that will fix her, there on the road's shoulder. It makes a cross. She can't not look at it as a cross. The line "recovering catholic." This makes her laugh. Then she thinks "jesus christ," then "goddamn it."

First crank. The muscle in her right arm pops up, ready. The chords in her neck tighten. Her left arm dulls over; memory. Year one. Face a little off of the pavement. Skin, she thinks. Up close like this the road looks like bumpy, black, magnified skin. She laughs hysterically until the traffic light changes and he has grabbed her by the scruff—collar—something and yanked her back into the car. She still has vomit smear around her mouth and she continues to laugh her ass off. Seven hundred dollars, he says, you can't just carry your money around in your pockets like that. He says, look at it, it nearly fell out of your shirt pocket into the street there, it's got barf on it, for christ's sake, then where would you be? Jesus. She's still laughing. She can't help it.

At the next light she opens the door and leans out again to puke, or laugh, or ride.

Year two. I'll pay you two hundred fucking dollars to kiss that guy on the mouth. She's waving the cash in one hand like a gray-green fan, steering with the other. Her lover and some guy they picked up on the side of the road. She's bored. They've been driving for two hours in some shit-sack place in Texas. Flat flat flat fuck this state she is thinking. Pancake flat. Hand splat on pavement flat. She nearly distracts herself right out of the car thinking lines. Where do you come up with this shit, he asks, to which she replies, with tongue. The two men look at each other innocently. They are high. Childlike. They are more beautiful than is humanly, manly possible. She wants it. She wants his mouth on his mouth in her rear view. She wants man on man wet like that. She pulls the car over into dirt and scrub and the lost dry heat of endless sky. She gets out of the car. Her boots crunch-print. She makes tracks on that land. She leans against the red metal smooth as a drive-in movie. She smokes. She waits for them. She waits for them to meet a woman with a want bigger than Texas. Her cunt throbs. Spit fills her mouth. The crook of her left arm begs. She squeezes it there hard enough to leave red prints.

Yes, they do. Then they split her money. Then they all fix there in the shade of the open trunk, wide open as a mouth. Then her eyes wild like fire. Then closed. Her arm lax. Her mouth opening. Her desire a flooded desert. Smile float teeth vertebrae melt.

Year three. They do not speak of it except to call it "the incident." The incident starts out around nine p.m. which is nine p.m. exactly the same as any other night. She is at a bar which is known to him, as her body is known to him, her mind, her movements, even her mindless desires. Shooting around like marbles. Blue quickening. At nine p.m. he is understanding that their arguments leave a mark. A sting over his heart, a scar, something. He places his hand there. Over his heart. Nothing nothing nothing beats back at him. Dull thudding. Even though he doesn't know for sure where she is he knows she is at this bar.

He is right.

As he walks in he is mesmerized by the smell and the dark and the red vinyl and the sticky black linoleum floor and the regulars and the band setting up and her hair, hanging behind her, a blonde mess. Each step he takes is his memory flashing an image at a time. His footsteps in his eyes walking up his own driveway. The windows of the car fogged up. The car seeming to move there in the driveway. His heart seizing. His anger welling up in his veins. He knows but doesn't, then does again. He opens the car door. A man is fixing her, but he is also fucking her, his dick is already sliding into her smooth as a needle into its waiting. The next image happens when he blinks, breaks the motion of things, his eyelids moving in slow motion, following his feet, dumb. He is grabbing the guy by the hair and yanking him out of the car. Another blink. Walking across the floor of a bar is exactly the same as walking across their front lawn. Stepping closer to her hair. Blonde mess. Grabbing her left arm. The needle ripping across her upturned flesh, ripping a second mouth open in the pale and infant-thin skin. Step and blink. Blonde mess. Her hair. The smell of her cunt, of her cum, of his. He feels as though he might vomit walking across the floor of the bar where she is sitting, all hair, all that blonde. Walking the play-by-play. She is laughing. But there is blood coming from her arm. Her left arm the bruise her left arm the poem her left arm their fucked-up love. Emergency. Emergency room. Blonde mess. Her blood cleaned up and put back into her, their love put back into her, her arm sutured, bandaged.

He is on her. His hand there in the bar. On her shoulder. Her hair. She spins a bit, then stops, since she knows it's him. Then she looks at the bar mirror which is him. They look at each other like that for a long minute. Then she pitches her drink in his face and leaves. It is unbelievably overdramatic. The words "hyperbole pick-up-sticks-fuck" knock around in her skull like dice in a cup in her leaving, though he doesn't know this precisely. He knows this dully.

He lets her.

He knows where she will go next. Her bandaged arm dangles from her shoulder like some new punctuation of a body.

She will go to a dance club next.

She does.

He finds her there hours later. She is dance-humping a woman with whom she has been lovers in their past. She is in full motion, sweat, pounding of sound, bodies beating each other for all they are worth. She is deaf with desire and wet movement. She is a blur. She is a smudge. She is smudging herself into moving particles, physics.

Someone outside of this motion grabs her arm in a sharp interruption. She knows the hand like the back of her hand. She is spun round to face him, and his face, and his ripping out of the room and outside, and her chasing him, and their yelling in a parking lot, and her pounding the metal of the car, and his throwing her against it, and his getting in to drive away from her, and her opening the passenger side door, and his yanking it closed against her, and her arm breaking there, blue, red, bone, her arm in the door, her arm their life, her bandaged arm shattering like sticks.

Year four. Road tripping. Somewhere near the coast. A roadside park. Redwoods and tree needles and California has a smell. Cooking up mushrooms in a cup-a-soup at a picnic table. Cross-country. Crossing country. Land masses.

Flight. Then their bodies begin to numb, they yawn, they laugh, colors change shape and little vague star-shapes clatter at the edge of their vision. They see three things.

A man who is drunk climbing up the side of the embankment there at the roadside park. He has a rainbow colored, crocheted hat on, rasta, and he has a sleeveless white t-shirt on, and he has on khaki-colored shorts, and he seems like a cartoon of some sort. He has a long black ponytail and pock-marked skin. He looks a hundred years older than he is. He climbs like some animal, gets very far up the hill. Pulling on shrubs and branches and shit. They are mesmerized. The man getting smaller and smaller up the hill like that. It is easy to be hypnotized by this. She laughs smally. Under her breath almost. He puts his hand under her shirt. Cups her breast, then puts her tit between his thumb and forefinger. It feels to him like a ball bearing. He has no idea. Then the man loses his grip and tumbles slow motion Technicolor back down the hill, head over heels, all the way to the road where he lands with this weird splat noise. Or bone crash. Or something. Everyone, which is just the three of them, keeps still for about a minute. Then he gets up, the man stands and walks away like it's all the most normal thing in the universe.

They get their mountain bikes out and decide it is an excellent plan to ride them onto the freeway. On the freeway they see many colors shooting by like molecules or corpuscles or DNA strands.

After several hours and some food and some whiskey and an attempt at fucking that turns into a nap they come back to themselves. They get back into the car and drive. They play The Doors on the car CD player louder than shit. She is laughing. She has whiskey all over her body. She always was clumsy. Like a kid. They come around a little California coast turn in the road and everything stops. Cars ahead of them with their brake lights on like little beady animal eyes all in a row. There is an accident. They see the ambulance. They see guys with uniforms carrying a stretcher. They see broken glass scattered and smashed metal like a disgruntled face. They see a guy on the stretcher. His skin is more pale than 2% milk. He has an institutionally beige big neck brace on. There is blood and something the color of iodine all over him. His mouth, his eyes, have gone slack. As if everything had been driven out of him. His arm dangles off of one side of the stretcher. It looks bigger than it should. Like a crab claw. Jim Morrison belts it out. He feels he might pass out. She is laughing like a deer caught in the headlights. He wants to clock her one, but doesn't, instead he drives them slow as blood beyond this scene.

When they can see the ocean again, he says what the fuck are you laughing at? How is that funny? She says did you see his ribs? I swear to god they looked like they had exploded out of his chest and broken into wings, did you fucking see that? Glorious. And her head rocks back. And her eyes close. And her needing to say that. And her terrible beauty.

Year five.
As you know incarcerations.
As you know the roof of your own mouth.
As you know the fingers you use to touch yourself.
As you know what hurts and what you want to hurt toward pleasure.
As you know the stupid line that does not exist there.
As you know the spit in your mouth.
As you know going down on a woman. Age ten. Age twenty. Age thirty.
As you know his mouth will never be her mouth.
As you know his taste will never be hers.
As you know your teeth clenching, wishing, wanting, biting.

As you know driving a car very fast is the same as living a life.

As you know the scars you carry.

As you read the Braille of your own body, self inscription.

As you know the scripts we are given fold in on themselves: this is a woman.

As you know single malt scotch pooling in your mouth better than saliva.

As you know the word "want" as an entire lexicon.

As you know the weight of your left arm, the pull, the mastery of your right hand, the tubing in your teeth, the skill of your fingers at work, the flesh taking the stab, the vein pulsing toward rupture, the breathing jack-knifing in lungs, the cold air rushing up your throat, your skull, the sockets of your eyes, you nearly swallowing your own teeth, my god, the knowing, the rain let loose to pure body, her knowing, the first shot received as a child, the not crying, the fascination, the looking up with the eyes of a child at a beautiful man in white, his giving.

This is what a woman wants. This is wanting. Be good.

As you know sentences will fail.

As you know to take a needle and cum.

From that.

Need driving you.

Shooting.

Year six. Motherfucker. Mother. Fucker. The phrase "detox for recovering catholics." She laughs and laughs. They have given her a roommate with red hair. She wants her. She watches her in her sleep and masturbates under white sheets. Her hands alive and unflinching. The red-headed woman becomes her need. Her drive. She lunges, propels herself across their room, over linoleum and white, over sterile and clean too clean shock backed floors and walls.

Turns out the redhead is awake. Sweating. Corpse-like in a pool of herself. Breathing in rapid bursts. Her hands on fire or maybe just screaming. Her hair, screaming.

They nearly devour each other like animals locked up.

Next day they sit semi-circle with other women, black circles under every eye. Most are smoking. Legs thrown out in front of them at odd angles. Mouths, eyes, all saying resist resist resist. Hearts saying fuck you fuck you fuck you fast or slow.

She thinks goddamn it, then lines that mimic that phrase, such as dogs have it, go bang it, fuck bag it, gun big it. She laughs. Is there something funny, L? Did you have something to say? Do you think maybe laughter is your cover story? Huh? Let's hear about it. C'mon. Show us some guts. Take a risk for once in your life. Tell us something we don't know. You mad? You got some rage in you that you think is special? A counselor tries to draw her out.

Cunt throb it.

Hand ram it.

Lead blood it.

Goddamn it.

She is forced to stay an extra four months for carving the line "goddamn it" into her arm with a sharpened and sharpened pencil.

The lost year. She is in the parking lot of Our Lady of Little Flowers Church. She is sitting there dull and blood. She is there for a commitment ceremony. He asked, what's a commitment ceremony. She called him a dumb fuck. It's when two queer people want to love each other in public, motherfucker. He didn't say anything, then did. She'd been clean nine months. Does it mess with you? What? That she's marrying someone else? Someone not you? Or that you married me? Is that it? Was that it? Did that make you feel incarcerated or something?

All she hears in her head is blood pounding goddamn it goddamn it goddamn it driving her crazy, making her brain propel itself down the rivers of her body into the veins in her arm into lines like what is a woman what is a woman what is fuck.

Year eight. She is driving in the desert. For all she is worth. With her whole body. Her mind gone wild. Her hair like fire. Her cells dividing or raging. It could be rage or love or just plain need. She drives most of the year. Or at least it seems that way. That driving. Those tracks.

Year nine. To cause to be projected, to cause to fire, to kill by doing this, to wound by doing this, to put to death with a bullet as a punishment, to hunt, usually used with "away," "down," "out," or "off," to destroy or move with a projectile. To go quickly through, under, or over. To project something forward, out, towards. To direct with the rapidity of a moving bullet. To streak with another color or colors. To send down a chute. To drive in the direction of something. To put into action. To detonate. To photograph. To take the attitude of. To play. To arrive with great speed like a moving projectile, to grow quickly. To jut out. To propel. To increase in speed. To flash across the sky. To dart painfully in or through a part or parts of the body.

Year Ten. On the road's shoulder. One moment. Flat tire. Thought-fucked. Her arms changing a tire on an ordinary car. Then into her vision comes taillights and somebody pulling over. Was it her hair that drew them, driving out in blonde tracks against the sky? It is a man, she thinks, and then a beautiful man, his hair long and wind-blown, a man gets out of his car and from the knee down his legs get bigger and bigger. When he is a foot away from her he stops. Then and only then she looks up. Up from the black leather boot to the bottom cuff of his jeans up his shin to his knee to his thigh up his denim to his cock. Then up his belly his torso his collarbone she pictures under his t-shirt his jaw his mouth his eyes. His whole face. Then his lips. They could be anyone's lips. They could be hers.

"It looks like you could use" is all she hears.

She lets this man help her even though she doesn't need. His arms working are more beautiful than is humanly, manly possible. His hands. His arms. The insides of his arms. Then and only then she thinks: I remember the veins in his arms more clearly than his face.

When he is finished he says the line "do you want to score?"

Then and only then it hits her. Shoots through her. The past wants. Like the mouth salivating. Like the cunt begging. Like the weight of an arm. Like the next sentence. Like a faith that won't be arrested. The past breaks her body no matter what, moves her, projects her, propels her, speeds her. The past's needing. No stopping it. The past drives her open, unendingly, like

Chair

A dictionary begins when it no longer gives the meaning of words, but their tasks. Thus formless is not only an adjective having a given meaning, but a term that serves to bring things down in the world, generally requiring that each thing have its form. What it designates has no rights in any sense and gets itself squashed everywhere, like a spider or an earthworm. In fact, for academic men to be happy, the universe would have to take shape. All of philosophy has no other goal; it is a matter of giving a frock coat to what is, a mathematical frock coat. On the other hand, affirming that the universe resembles nothing and is only formless amounts to saying that the universe is something like a spider or spit.

—Georges Bataille

1. The grain swells. Since 1902. The oak fills the room, and the objects fill his vision, and his vision nearly pours out of the sockets of his eyes. Spit fills his mouth. He has purchased two chairs. He has put them in this room, his work room. They sit before him, asking.

A rope thick-bristled and raw as an arm half in his hand, half coiled on the floor. His own arm twitching in the faintest pulse imaginable before he moves.

Their backs face one another. Two arcs doubling. The wood curving in that impossible way that wood does. The velvet of the red seats sanguine beyond dried blood. Personless familiars. They sit dead in the way that chairs move us.

With the slowness of breath he laces the rope through the back arc of one, then the other. With the carefulness of a carpenter he swings his arm forward, back, forward, looking skyward; faith. With the skill of a man in the middle of his life he pitches the rope up and up and of course around a metal pipe jutting like pipes do from the ceiling. He has calculated the action in his mind. He has seen each second laying itself bare as if in an architectural diagram. He has considered every moment in excruciating detail. His hands are dirty. His fingernails lined with black. Splinters sting each palm without his notice. The rope hovers like an idea suspended like ideas do for a long second, then over the pipe, then drops back down to him as if he perfectly asked.

To lift the chairs. To watch them kiss themselves and knock wood against wood in a sound he has never heard before in his entire life, nor will. To witness their rising. Together. Forever like that. Tilted in against one another like some strange new species. Leaning taut like muscles or clenched teeth. The one against the other. Nearly unbearable.

Hand over hand and the biceps pulling like biceps do. His eyes lifted. Blue. His mouth open slightly. His lips wetted. His tongue against his front teeth barely like that. The chords in his neck straining but with ease. His jaw present. Their weight is not heavy. Simply weighted in the most remarkable way.

He has taken such care. Against the white wall, after the first day he saw them, before he spoke to the shop-keeper, moments after speaking to his wife (had he forgotten? Had he lost himself into a longing unnameable, some ache reaching for light? Her voice so familiar he no longer recognizes it, her thoughts dull as wood, her responses known to him like the back of his hand, repeating endlessly?), he has mounted a metal prong. When the chairs reach the ceiling (no, not the ceiling. Just under it. Like a word sent out to a listener doesn't meet them but comes as near as is possible to their own mouth), he pulls the rope toward the metal prong and laces it once, twice, three times, then drops the length of it to the floor. The rope thuds like a heart.

There will be no knot, no certain stability. There will be only this rope holding. He will work directly beneath them time and again. There will always remain the chance that they will fall, together like that, back to back, palm to palm, psalmed, there will always remain his not knowing, his longing, his wonder lifting.

2. A relative silence settles. All the stupefied glances are arrested. The image seizes its onlookers. Look. Seated as they are, static and in the dark, a dark which would so easily overtake them that it is laughable, they convulse. Is it agony, well no. But they mistake it for agony. Look. A woman as common as a sentence stretches herself out naked before them. Her back that of eastern European women, longer and without the curves one expects. Her ass white rising screened. Her cleft black and the wiry hairs magnified to monstrous proportions. Her head severed—not part of the picture, is it? The heads of the viewers repugnant as a thousand worms butting their way through dirt, emerge in the dark, pulse toward the screen. One feels compelled to spray gasoline on the lot of them. Are they holding back pathetic cries? One can only imagine the overwrought pathos of this moment. My god. Teeth bite into lips. Mouths so agitated they are comic. Contracted by strangulation. The eyes have it. Roaring laughter that no one hears. Contracted by death; after all, don't they want to watch this woman's body in time and space? Who among us will yell "FIRE!"

3. A little girl coming out of a theater. Her brother has taken her to the movies so that he can feel up his girlfriend there in the dark. She has been terrified. Terrified by a family,

terrified by speech, by speaking in public, by that thick
mucous forming at her mouth when people are watching
her attempt to talk, terrified by the eyes and the watching
and the voyeuristic cannibalism that seems to never end,
terrified by her brother's knowing, his hands, terrified by
her own want, her crotch throbbing in ways she cannot
name, her body making her cry, terrified by images big as
buildings overwhelming her to the point of disembodiment,
terrified of her own hands finding her pre-pubescent cunt,
terrified by her mouth filling with spit, terrified of the theatre chairs cupping her like a hot palm, terrified of her own
courage. Her brother's girlfriend is red and sweaty and her
hair is messed up. Her lipstick is all over her face. There was
a moment in the film where she saw her ass, glowing in the
dark, and she thought of apes, and she thought she might
pass out or vomit. When it is over the murderous crowd
comes spilling out of the theatre into daylight. Everyone's
eyes hurt. She rushes to a woman her mother thank you god
and wraps her little arms around her waist and buttocks.
She begins to cry while her face is buried in the woman's
crotch. She hears, "Hello little girl, are you lost?" She thinks
and thinks and thinks and then looks up to see a woman
she has never seen before in her life. She thinks and thinks
and the only sentence that happens in her brain like some
ticker tape is "are you my mother? are you my mother?"
Little bird gone crazy.

4. In this room the skin bulges of an ankle-thick push between twine and the wooden leg of a chair making a question: how long?

5. A small red wooden stool. That of a child. A dead one.
    She squats, her ass comes down onto it. She is naked. She
is drunk. The stool wobbles underneath her weight, underneath years, underneath a body thudding and swollen. In

front of her a mute television set, exactly the height of a child. She reaches through the space between them and turns it on. She pushes another button on a VCR, and an image appears before her there on the screen. It is as if the television has given her the image.

She pisses. Slowly. Just sitting there. The piss running down her leg. Down the leg of the stool. She is lost in her watching.

She does not cry.

A little girl in near sepia tones (wasn't her husband there? she cannot remember. wasn't there a video camera? who captured this image?) twirling and twirling in circles. Running sideways. Berserk in her girlhood. Little grass hula skirt. Little topless doll. Little tits. Little mouth almost gagging from laughing. The girl stops dead in her tracks, does an almost obscene little wriggling of her hips, some idea of a hula dance, from movies, from pictures, from god knows what, then speeds out of the frame like thought killed.

The drunk woman stops the image's flow. Rewinds. Does it again.

Again.

Again.

A small red stool.

A small red stool.

A small red stool.

Push play.

6. In the film *Death and the Maiden*, there is a point during which Sigourney Weaver has duct-taped Ben Kingsley to a chair in her living room. The characters are reenacting a reverse torture scene. To move the plot of a woman tortured toward its desire: to torture the torturer. To extract a confession.

The chair is a prop.

A prop is a stage object that supports the drama.

If the audience suspends their disbelief, the chair transforms itself in time and space. If the audience is left unconvinced, the chair is silly and imaginable in anyone's living room.

In the film *Romeo is Bleeding*, Lena Olin sits in a chair and spreads her legs so that her cunt can be seen/scene. Her nationality keeps slipping; she is what we want her to be in a million ways. Her severed arm our severed arms. Her mouth opening like a country.

In the film *Exotica*, Atom Egoyan has the male lead (primary actor, financial draw) sit in a chair immobile while a child-stripper dances excruciating close to his body. His hands on his thighs. His mouth open. His mind seated. Torture.

In the film *Barbarella*, Jane Fonda is trapped inside of a science fiction sexual orgasm chair. This is before her politics come.

In the film *Breaker Morant*, two men, mutated soldiers lost, are executed—shot through the chest—while seated in chairs.

In my kitchen I jack my father off while he sits in a chair, my hand smally domestic, the back of the chair holding his back, the legs of the chair forgiving his weight, the wood of the chair blonde, the hair of the girl blonde, the room magnified to cinematic proportions.

How to Lose an Eye

Now he thinks in corporeal commands: *Do not rub from the nose toward the side of your face. Always wipe toward the nose in a horizontal direction.*

His eyes are closed. No. His eye. He picks up the phone. He dials. His skin is too hot against the headpiece. A voice says, "Hello," then he speaks, then "Jackson?" This voice resting him. His heart beating out thank god thank god thank god. The voice says, "Where are you?" He responds, "Can I see you tonight?" Then he nearly passes out from an ordinary sentence.

He does not know how to explain why he needs to be in the car. He thinks up a hundred absurd errands a day so that he can be driving around until dark. Maybe it's that he needs that movement to hold him in place. When he sits inside his house even the air looks empty. And lopsided. The whole world looks slightly off. As if it is not a change in him at all. As if it is instead the world that has changed its angle of vision, closed in on itself, de-focused. Isn't that the damnedest thing? Perhaps the single line of a road is the only thing that will ever make sense to him again.

It makes him horny to drive to Mary's house. They have never been lovers. They will never be lovers. He doesn't fuck women. Not that he hasn't, just that he doesn't. Mary makes him horny because the way of their knowing each other has lasted twenty years. Because she is a big woman,

Amazonian, man-like except that this makes her unusually feminine. In that European kind of way. Or something. Because she gives him back rubs that last two days. Because she can't cook and he cooks for her and it makes her cry to eat. Because they are both knee deep in their lives and have no idea how to proceed. Because they both ended up in California after swearing not to. Because she will not leave him, ever, did not, in the hospital, slept in a chair, like a woman waiting in a movie, exactly like the image of a woman in a movie. Because she has little scars all over her body from a car accident years and years ago, little glowing white feathers covering her torso. Because their suffering is stronger than love. Because she will look him in the eye. Because she is the only human he has seen in months who will do that.

His cock hard.

The orb itself has no surrounding connective tissue context. A CONFORMER made of silicone is placed inside the socket following surgery to maintain orbit volume and to help form cul-de-sacs or lid pockets that will hold the eye in place.

His driving down her dead end, his hearing the car door metal shut whack sound, his feet carrying him down a path he could walk with his eyes closed, his knocking on her door, her letting him in, their kissing, their looking at each other, smiling, then her eyes traveling down his body, then her saying, "My god, look at that!" Their laughing their heads off.

Their eating the pesto and pasta he cooks. Their getting high after dinner and his taking his patch off. Her fingers soft as whispers, his flesh hollow. Their watching videos until 3 a.m.—*Red, White, Blue*—their falling asleep, tangled bodies on the couch. Her saving his life, him saving hers, and no one seeing it.

The colored spot goes up, under the upper lid upon inser-
tion.

He wouldn't want to lose his way, after all. That's why he
bought the maps in the first place. Six of them. Funny thing
was, each of them was slightly different than the other. Now
why was that? One would think there would be some kind
of consistency or standardization. Computer-generated im-
aging that proved something. But he'd find a street on one
and not another. He'd find a bridge on one and not another.
He'd find sights listed on one and not another.

He bought the maps as part of THE PLAN. THE PLAN
was to drive cross-country to get his mojo, his self-worth,
his chutzpah back. To find it. To get in a car and goddamn
remember a self. He and Mary had been trying to think up a
"healing journey." Mary had heard from her therapist that
"healing journeys" were important. Mary was going on and
on about a possible trip to Europe, and he spit out, "What
about a road trip, what if I took myself, by myself, on a road
trip?" And Mary had said that's pretty loaded, Jackson. How
would you feel about being in a car for something like that?
I mean, stuck in a car for that long? And he'd said, I love
cars. I love road trips. I've always felt more myself inside
driving—inside movement. She'd paused knowingly then.
Then she'd said perhaps that's just right. Perhaps revising
the story in a ritual like that—driving—would be just the
thing. Then she'd looked at him eye to eye and said "go."
He'd felt for an instant like they were in some kind of intimate mucous bubble where no one could see them.

That's when they came up with THE PLAN. THE PLAN
was to drive from Seattle to California to Arizona to New
Mexico to Texas, through the rest of those southern states to
Key West, all the way not stopping, to there. And to film it, to
capture it a frame at a time and replace the nightmare with
something real. Like that. In a car not the car that had killed

Michael and not the car that had taken his sight but a car he
had since any of that. Beyond the horizon of any of that.

*After you wash and rinse your hands, lift the upper lid with
the thumb or forefinger of one hand. Next, slide under the
upper lid and, while holding it in place, pull down on the
lower lid.*

Waking up in the night, cold sweat, like a big fleshy cliché
of a self. Did his whole life leak out of the black socket that
night, or only part of it? His memory bends in on itself like a
video stuck on pause. Even when he shuts his eyes as tightly
as is humanly possible, the images continue, perhaps stronger than ever, sometimes so fast he cannot watch, sometimes so slowly he cannot breathe.

In the morning he makes a list of things to pack, even as
his mind, his sight, his body are all ahead of him. The list
runs and runs with or without him. Boxerstenjeansfour
tshirtstensockstensweatersandfleecethreeleatherjacketone
sunglassesbrooksbrothersbuttondownsgapthreerunning
shortsniketwocapstwoaftershavedeodorantelectricrazor
attachmentsforbeardandnosehairstoothbrushtoothpaste
travelsizeshampooandcremerinsel'occidentlotionandbath
milkfirstaidkitwaterscotchsinglemaltfivebottlesjohnsonsbaby
shampooqtipsmoneycamerafilmeyes.

In the afternoon he packs the car. Mary comes over to
help. Then Mary leaves, and as she is waving good-bye from
her car he thinks, she looks a little like a bird, some great
prehistoric bird dipping its wing before it builds the speed
up enough for flight.

In the evening, when it is cool and the road whispers its
blue-black beg, he drives.

*Do not be alarmed by tears and secretions. Simply wipe to-
ward the nose with a tissue or warm wash cloth to remove*

secretions. You can also use Johnson's baby shampoo and Q-tips for cleaning dried secretions from the margins. If any thick secretions or excessive tearing occur call the emergency hotline.

Inside motion is the only place he feels normal. Driving is best, next to that, swimming. There is something about the way a car holds you. Something about shutting the doors and the cup of the seat like a hand and the steering wheel presenting itself to you as if you could control things like direction and speed. Speed comforts him too, as if all of existence could be reduced down to that one element, as if speed named a fundamental feature of existence.

With water it is floating. The way water carries a body. Weightless.

At first the road trip is like a photo essay. He keeps having feelings like now I am crossing the border between Washington and Oregon. Now I am on the Coast Road. Now I am changing speed zones, highway to suburban area to city and out and up and faster again. He keeps having feelings like the same landscape is passing by for the second, third, fourth, fifth time. Only small set changes take place. Then geographic ones, the hills a little more browned from sun, the trees less evergreen and more eucalyptus or palm. Smells seem more telling. He is driving and California has a smell, orange trees and asphalt. He is driving and the hills give way to ocean, sea air and exhaust. He is driving and memory moves his sight, his hearing, his heart beating, as he leaves the west coast the windshield is a giant body…no, it is simply the California hills giving way like great shoulders into the Southwest desert or the well of the small of a back.

But the body filling the windshield before him is always the same. No matter what he stops to take pictures of all he hears is the clicking of the camera, its eye blinking machine-like, its shutter controlling light and speed. No matter the stilled shot, red earth of New Mexico, redwoods of California, road signs and vistas, moonlight on an ocean, all he sees is Michael thrown from the car, his shirt ripped open, his browned biceps and chest cut clean through, Michael perfect, Michael perfectly still, Michael shot from the car onto the road, his eyes open for the rest of his life.

It is during the drive that he realizes the film inside the camera has pictures already burned onto it. You know how the camera gets left sitting around, dormant, static, waiting for its next series to be completed. You know how you get the film developed and the time of things is suddenly out of whack...Christmas up against summer, installing the new entertainment center against the grain of a black tie event, as if you were the actors that would animate the new TV, VCR, and DVD player. It is in some moment of driving past image after image of scenery that he is seized with the fact clear and cutting that there are pictures of Michael somewhere on the roll. At least three.

His mind numbs itself. He considers blinding the camera with his fist. He considers throwing it out the window of the car. He ends up putting it between his legs, its lens pointed up to him, its glass eyeing him questioningly.

He wakes up in a hotel in Ashland, Oregon, crying. Or he was crying in his sleep, and then he woke, but his tears are still present, salty and damp. His eye still cries, what is he supposed to think of that? He just lies there in the dark thinking I am not blind. He isn't exactly thankful, he's just thinking it in a kind of ordinary sense. He looks at the objects in the room. They are like shadows of themselves in the darkness. A chair. Mirror. His bags. The window curtains. The television. He grabs the remote and clicks the television on. He holds the remote to his dead eye without thinking. He rubs it down some into the hole without thinking. He touches it to his mouth without thinking. He falls asleep with the little electronic gizmo tightly fisted and close to his cheek.

He wakes in a hotel in Tucumcari, bolting upright, tight like a car jack, his teeth clenched. His eyes are closed but he can still see the flashing red lights of the ambulance, or the fire truck, or the cop car, or all of them, or just retinal splashes gone berserk, or blood in his eye, or how the hell should he know?

He wakes up in a hotel in Pensacola. He left the window open all night so that he could hear the sea. He is smiling a little. He gets up to pee, pees, looks in the bathroom mirror. Mild nausea. Still. He looks down at his eye in a hotel glass filled with saline solution. It looks back. His chest tightens, he does a mini-breathing exercise until it loosens again. He leaves the bathroom, turning off the light, leaving the eye submerged and displaced.

Too much handling can cause socket irritation.

There is an oyster bar that a friend told them about called One-Legged Pete's. They should go there for the view, the scene, and for these big buckets of crab legs and suck so sweet your lips ache oysters. All the double entendres which used to be playful and sexy lodge in his jaw like nails now. He gathers up the pictures he has taken so far, his camera, and his wallet. He goes back into the bathroom and rips off about a two-inch long, two-inch wide piece of white surgical tape. He places it where his eye should be.

It is not necessary for you to wear a bandage.

At the bar he thinks how right the friend is. He thinks how much Michael would have liked it, Michael the more outgoing one, the more playful one, the one with the *GQ* smile, Michael the already tanned don't need to go to fucking Florida for that one, Michael the well hung, the fucking god in bed, the one who never cried. Blue eyes. Two. Perfect as water. He looks out at the ocean. He can smell it. He can hear it. In his mind's eye he can picture them swimming in it.

At the bar he gets his pictures out. He looks at them closely, one at a time. Whatwhatwhat has he been taking pictures of? All he can see are things one would see from a moving vehicle. Things that would be on the side of a road. Road signs, big farm fields, lines of trees. Shots of hills with telephone wires decapitating them. Images of strip malls and gas stations and truck stops. One in particular baffles him. It's of license plates for christ's sake. A line of them. VGB 197, New Jersey. PLC 306, Colorado. VMV 000, California. HOT ROD, Nevada. Is HOT ROD why he took the picture? Was he drunk? Possessed by his lover's juvenile sense of humor? He doesn't remember. He suddenly remembers a conversation they had…how lucky they were. That neither of them were sick. Nor were they likely to be. That both had been careful and precise sexual partners before they got together. That both were young. That both were ready to commit and make a life together stretching out like the fingers of a human hand. He is seized in the gullet enough that he cannot order a bucket of crab legs. Nor can he suck down any oysters. He wants to wade into the sea up to his eyes and cry.

Make certain to use all of the medications prescribed to you.

Though he has considered turning back every single day since he left, just as he has considered suiciding every single day since the accident, he keeps going, and a day comes when he is in Key West. The heat of Florida has dulled his senses. He has the permanent taste of scotch lining the insides of his mouth. He can taste it with his tongue every time he presses it against his inner cheek. He checks into a beautiful white hotel named The Conch House. The linens smell heavily of fabric softener in a way which comforts him. The walls are white. The furniture is white. Everything is clean like brushed teeth or sheets.

He sits out on the pool deck in a white wicker chair. A hotel attendant brings him a piña colada. He spikes it further with scotch. It suddenly tastes like shit but he doesn't care, he is relaxed and drowsy, his eyelids are heavy with almost sleep. He is wearing his eye. His camera is in his lap. He has in mind a short nap and then as the sun sets a walk down the main drag for photos. Rhythmically breathing in the thick wet heavy of Key West he comes close to dozing.

An enormous splash snaps his lids up to reveal a beautiful blurry sea creature; no, it is a statue fallen into the pool; no, it is a man-boy tanned and slippery surfacing from a dive. His hair is black and sheened as a record album. His skin the color of Albuquerque sand. His eyes unbearably onyx and open. If there is something he does not want a photo of, an image of, it is this boy. If ever something could be violently true, it is that a photo of this boy might kill him. Taking the picture alone might be as if someone had shot him in the face. He is overcome with this feeling. He is paralyzed, pinned and stunned in a white lawn chair. It is horrible, this beauty. This magnificent. It is a violence. He begins to cry, soon he is crying uncontrollably. Worse, the man-boy sees him and begins to move toward him. He honestly thinks if the man-boy comes much nearer to him he might need medical attention. As the man-boy's body magnifies, as he comes closer and closer, soon as large as a cinematic close-up, his lips tortuously full, even the bridge of his nose excruciatingly perfect, as the creature approaches he begins to surrender. His skin goes slack and his jaw gaws some and his heart stops jack-knifing and it is then that his camera slips to the concrete with a little cracking tink noise.

"Oh man, you dropped your camera…here, let's see if it's got any damage…lemme wipe my hands off first…there. Let's have a look at it."

The youth turns it over and over in his large hands like a sunken treasure.

"Oh Jesus. I think the lens is cracked. That's terrible. I think that might be really expensive to replace. Look, I'll go ask up front if they know of a repair shop. I'm certain they can find you one. Wait here."

And with that the boy is gone, or is it a man, or is it his mind trying to kill him?

If too much time passes before fitting, the socket may begin to shrink and it may become more difficult to achieve a satisfactory cosmetic and functional result. If too little time elapses, not enough healing has occurred to achieve a proper fit.

Back in his hotel room he locks the door. He shuts the drapes. He turns off the light. He doesn't ever want to see the boy again. He doesn't want his camera to exist. He hopes it spontaneously combusts. He'd rather die than have to open the door to the knocking brown hand of the beautiful boy holding the idiotic and horrible camera out to him, saying, there, I had it fixed, it works like brand new, now you can take all of the photos you want while you are here, and would you like to have a drink to celebrate the camera's repair, the hotel has a bar, just a drink, perhaps dinner if you are free, if not, that's fine, just thought sharing company might be nice tonight, what with the camera incident and all, and where did you say you were from? He actually catches himself looking at the back wall of his hotel room for an alternate exit. All he can see is the mirror and himself staring lopsidedly back at him.

What was he thinking? He was not ready for a trip like this. He was not fit for human interaction. He is suddenly surprised he was able to drive the car this distance without some terrible repeat crash. The room spins some and he feels as if he might faint. He makes his way to the scotch and pours a glass quickly, then sucks it down. He reaches up and jams his forefinger into his eye and pry-sucks the eye out, it tumbles to the carpet. He picks it up and puts it in his mouth. He considers swallowing it.

What it comes down to is this: he feels trapped inside this white room with a dead eye and a self he cannot bear and set of memories more alive than his present. He feels as if the boy will come back to kill him at any moment. He feels as if there is no escape. He thinks I will die here one way or another.

Hours pass. He's no idea how many.

Things become darker.

Of course eventually there is a knock at the door. He looks at the door, one-eyed and weak. He goes to the door. He opens it.

The flash is more white than the mind can imagine, white like all color in the universe collecting in the pinhole of that moment.

"Surprise."

The shutter releases him, things go back to gray and still life for an instant. It is the boy. He is smiling in the way that boys do. What can only be called a grin.

"It was no trouble, no trouble at all. There happened to be a used lens at a shop just around the corner. I know a lot about cameras. I got you a good deal. But now, I'm afraid, you owe me dinner."

The boy stands there more innocent than the present. Something happens in the frame of the door there. Something he can't quite understand. It is as if his memory releases itself from his brain, his entire skull. Like it pours out of the hole in his head. Like it could do that. It is then as if he is in a dream, for all of his movements follow the boy's words. The boy has taken his picture in Key West, Florida. In the doorway of The Conch House. The boy has repaired his camera. The boy wants dinner. He gives up entirely.

After dinner they walk along the night beach with their pants rolled up at the ankle. Eventually they undress and slide into the black water, warm as the body's fluids, salty as tears. They float on their backs. He looks up at the roof of the world and thinks this is exactly what it looks like when you close your eyes. Only the stars are different.

Store in water or saline solution.

The next day he wants to be in his car, but differently. It is dawn. He dresses and leaves the room. He goes to his car. He takes his camera. He drives his car down to the beach. No one is there. He keeps driving. He drives onto the sand, even though cars are not allowed. He keeps driving. He drives up to the lip of the sea. Then in. Slowly and without alarm. Only a little ways, until the wheels are submerged. He opens the car door and steps out. He leaves the car there like that, the camera in the driver's seat.

He thinks in a day or two the boy will leave. He thinks he will sell his car and live on insurance money there in Key West for as long as he can. He thinks he will leave the camera just as it is, with his picture forever inside it. He thinks he might grow a beard, perhaps even wear a patch. He thinks it will be all right to go this way. He thinks it will be all right to live in a kind of sleep, or short-sightedness, in a place where the road ends in the sea, as if its motion could be cupped forever, since any other life at all will drive him to his end.

Signification

1. Everything unnamed. Lights outside a window at night. A small desk with a woman; still life. A persimmon tree, stones in a wall older than memory. The word "Etruscan" before her as an object, not speech. The word for night. The word for love. This language could be the valley below her. Her body never inside of it. What is inside? What outside? Without language everything returns to its object status. Imagination returns. Wonder. Huge. Violent. Like a child's.

Outside the window is night. Into the night tiny lights at the base of mountains. Behind the lights the houses of people she will never know, rooms she will never enter, laughter not her own or anyone's, ever. And in the rooms unknown echoes of the breath of sleeping bodies. And in their sleep how intimately close they are to her. It is nearly unbearable. How close they are in their utter distance. Nearly inside her skin. Her thoughts have never been so clichéd as this. She is more American than is possible.

2. A body embodied by body. In her belly language doubles, turns, breathes in water. What is a sentence there? Before language? If she is walking up and down streets older than the history of her own country, trying to keep her balance, looking up now and again at the Madonna with child etched in almost every wall, carrying Catholicism dead in her next

to a new life, walking inside of religion born into the very ground of this city, her breathing caught tight and high in her rib cage like a small bird's, her heart engorged like a fist, her spine still electric from his cock entering her from behind the night before, her mouth carrying the taste of chocolate, her hair wetted from rain and cold, her realization that she has never eaten a persimmon, barely knows what it is, though she is haunted by a poem carrying that title, her knowing that the first persimmon she will put in her mouth will be in January and entirely accidental and in a country where suddenly it seems persimmons must originate (how could they not fill the window, precede the mountains, glow like sex against the blue gray bruise of a sky storming), the hands of her first husband more memorable than his name, how her second husband drank wine as if it was all of their love, her dead child, her present child swelling like a too-ripe fruit, the way her present husband stares so hard into her eyes she feels she may explode—all her memories and her entire present tingling at the surface of her skin, undoing ordinary mind patterns, ordinary logics of the body walking, sending grammar out and across great masses of land to its scattered past, if she is all that, who is she? What is her name in a country whose language is foreign to her? In a country that would name her foreign? What is a sentence?

3. It is not her age that ages her. It is hearing sentences that she has heard before coming out of different mouths. It is the redundancy of speaking. It is the lie we tell ourselves about our own differences. It is the way body after body moves through life after life claiming originality and failing and falling and denying that. One would need to invent a new language to achieve the difference we all claim keeps us alive. Who among us would invent such a language? America is this. The inability to invent languages. Or: the ability to reduce all languages, all differences, all intimacies,

all acts of making, all suffering, to a single word. Without history.

A series of nights is coming like the structure of a new belief system. They are accompanied by specific affect: her tears. It is almost as if she cannot stop crying. She who never cries. Epic. Or biblical. Practically ridiculous.

The first night she cries because he has said: "I can't be around you right now." Right off the bat, upon their arrival, getting out of the rental car after the drive from the airport to the house they have rented. He says "you are mean and cold." She has no idea if he is speaking to her or to some genetic memory of his first wife, a woman from this country. It is possible. Both of them are so recently emerged from divorces it is nearly violent. Or he may be speaking to his mother or sister, the women that raised him. Somehow, and isn't this true of everything in the universe, some…how…his anxiety about driving a rental car in a foreign country transfers onto her reading the directions. Though she has read them precisely and calmly, she is certain of that. Though she had thought on the ride that they were "in it together" because she still has not fully learned that he cannot be "in" anything with anyone. Somehow some deep betrayal from his past or his DNA or his cosmic paths duplicating themselves has left him forever orbiting around a center. Still, what he says rips at her skin. He has looked inside of their love and broken through the membrane that holds their forming child inside of her. (Of course this is not the case. This is not the truth. He is simply tired from the flight, from the drive, from carrying luggage, from trying to take care of their journey, it is ordinary tension, ordinary stress, ordinary speech between people, all of which she knows and knows and knows. This is a relationship. This is the mood and ego of a man. This is a man and a woman speaking. Nothing more.) Her mind though is racing like a child's, it has regressed, it happened the moment she saw a land mass not her own from the window of the plane, it is always immaculate like that. And since her mind is racing in that way, her desire is out of whack as well. She wants the first night to be singular and new. She wants his first words in this new place to be beautiful and like a gift. She wants his love to surround her to the point of drowning. She is absurd in her wanting.

The second night she cries the first time because the sun coming down through the window breaks into hues that she has never seen before. (This is not true; she cries because he says: "Jesus Christ I don't even believe we'll last a year or two." No. She cries because he says: "Maybe we should be friends since we can't seem to fucking sustain ourselves beyond an hour or two." The intimacy of a couple capable of hurling itself like a comet endlessly through time. In her mind they burn up in the atmosphere, love's heat destroying matter.) This does not seem possible; she is forty years old. Surely she has seen the sky enough. And yet. It is so beautiful it is painful. It is so overly romanticized in her vision it is painful. It is so unsentenceable it is painful. It is the torture of beauty. It has always been the torture of beauty. We have never named it and we have believed it to be named endlessly. What does she do? She takes a photograph. Stunning in its stupidity.

The second night she cries the second time because the walk that they take down to the town square at night breaks (Or is it her inability to believe anyone would ever find her beautiful? The word itself glances off her body, crashes into the walls of the city. Isn't beauty always a dead object? Or if not dead, lost to us at some great distance? Isn't beauty the word we use when we fail to name something?) her. The

white lights strung in hanging arcs down each alley. The way
he holds her hand and wants to take her picture. How his
eyes are the entire world, how he has become all of her
experience right then, he is the whole country, his name dissolves, his body is in the movements and smells and colors of
the night, the streets, the lights, the vendors, the taste of wine
in her mouth, the entire night sky up from the rooftops, she is
lifted like that, she is so in love it is sacred. She is so in love it
is an endless repeatable sentence: "I love you" like time or
space refusing boundaries. Exactly like anyone.

The third night she cries from fear. It is not the fear of a
present moment. It is all the fear from her whole life and
from his as if painted on a wall before her. Again, it begins
in ordinary speech, in the act of lovers. He says: "It's ethno-
centric. You have to at least try. Go in there and ask for
some stamps." He is (Of course on one plane of existence
he is again, right. It makes no logical sense, she knows other
languages, has used them in other countries, she has always
been unusually skilled at picking them up. People are even
jealous of her knowledge, the speed with which she understands and lives things. Aside from her shyness—the kind
that kept her from speaking at all until she was twelve, and
who would count that now at her age—aside from that,
there is no reason. Is there?) irritated by her embarrassment.
Is it him telling her to (Here she hears the father too much.
Too loud. Again and again. Paralysis.) do it? She does not
know the word for the word "afraid." More than she is afraid
of speaking this language she does not know, she is afraid
of their lives. The word for their lives is unborn as yet. Unspoken. She is seized with an idea: she is waiting for their
lives to enter speech.

4. Inside of her mouth his tongue. Inside of her mouth her
own teeth. Biting a pulpy fruit in another country. Inside of

her mouth all the things she has ever said. All the things she will never say. All of language, born or not.

5. To what do we owe the present? He is talking about how they met. He says: "I loved you the first moment I saw you, even as I did not want to. And at the coffee shop. I didn't want to." (She knows that this is not true. He has changed the "moment" of love several times. It seems to get earlier and earlier. She wonders if it will soon travel to before she was born, genetic or cosmic or wombed. She wonders if he is trying to bring the past back in order to animate the present. She knows that he is worried that the present will not be sustainable. She knows because she is older than he is. A decade. A history. She remembers having the same fear. What moves us makes us.) While he is speaking and kissing her she is thinking about art. (Of course she is moved by his tenderness and love. Of course. Her body too responds, her nipples always harden, the small of her back and up through her spine whispers, her cunt aches for him, only for him.) She is thinking about how art has made history into a visible story. She is thinking that there isn't a word for that, though we have come up with many words. In the artistic history of representations of Christ (the infant) with Mary (the mother) we have one of the most stunning visual epics of all time. Look through the ages. Changes in forms, in perspectives, colors, materials, patrons, the way her breast appears, the way the infant's image takes on meaning after meaning, until there is an erotics between the breast and the infant. An entire belief system is born (He pinches her nipple between his thumb and forefinger. Her breast ignites from the inside out. He fingers her clit. He makes her come in those two small gestures between his fingers. She convulses, her uterus contracts. He asks her to suck his nipple. While she is handling his cock she does, she mouths his nipple, she is curled up against him fetally, his head rocks back, small pearls of

cum are born at the tip of his cock); in some images Mary's
tender hand seems to fondle the infant penis.

6. She had not meant to mention the friends so late in the
story. There was a point at which they were more present in
her mind. Back when a number of her childish desires had
accumulated in a heated swarm like a jarful of bees. Back
before the actual first day of being in the new country, she
had storied the friends crossing paths with the lovers and in
that interstice wild new intimacies they hadn't a language
for would get born. Kinds of love uncontained by America,
by the smallness of all their lives. Like books and epics. Like
myths and frescoes. She saw almost by firelight the glow of
them all merging and swelling in ways that changed them
all forever. Even now if she closes her eyes she can bring
the image back.

If she is not a child in these out of whack desires then perhaps just a nut case. What kind of idiot clings to such absurd
visions of the coming future? What kind of present does she
experience that she believes and believes in these possibili-
ties when their falling is inevitable? There is narrative and
then there is her life. The one she cannot live with and the
other cannot live without her. Tragic. If she weren't so stupid and deluded she'd be tragic.

Here is what actually happens. The friends are immediately
taken aback by the silent, angry, defensive nature of her
lover. This is their first impression: they've known no one
like him, this man who rarely speaks and whose entire body
radiates a kind of stone wall encircling being (but this is not
true, not at all, for the friends already carry a primary wounding. Her previous husband's selfishness and drunkenness
and lying. Even though his charisma and playfulness man-
aged to seduce them, seduce them all, in the end they were

each tortured for the sin of loving him. Why, it was just last Christmas, wasn't it, in a different country, her desire for them to spend Christmas there, to make the ornaments by hand, to cook and fuck and make and live there in that country not America, and now the desire refusing to die, or the story refusing to end or the sentence doubling back the way language does...relentless). From the first car ride from one city to another. They tell her later that the first car ride was excruciating (This is true—they actually use that word) and that it characterized the holiday from the get-go. They do not understand how it is that her lover can be such an angry and defensive man. They find his silences and disinterest in everything they say and do to be offensive. They think he considers them to be morons. They think he wants them to go away immediately, and since they will not, he will will them out of existence a day at a time. One of the friends says: "It's as if we have intruded upon your honeymoon. Intruded into a space so private as to be obscene and violent. It's as if we're being punished." (This has some truth to it...their lives are indeed privatized in ways that must seem oppressive to everyone around them. And it is also true that they, the lovers, are nearly incapable of being out in the world with other people. It's as if their being only emerges in a room at a time, alone, eroticized. In those rooms everything is possible. After all, their love is new. When they take that love out into the world it is as if all the oxygen is consumed by fire.)

In her other ear is her lover, telling her that the friends understand nothing of their lives together. That the friends have no respect for or interest in their coming lives together, their love, what new forms may emerge from their making. He says: "They don't value what we are together." He says: "They only know you as the woman from their lives, from that story. They don't want you to be anything else." (This also seems true, but differently. And the question remains, who is he, in this country the country his ex-wife was born in, this country he lived in with her, this woman, this country whose language he learned, made a life as if it would story-over everything and hold? In those moments he is speaking to her in sentences which nearly break her, which wife is he speaking to? The past wife, or the present life?)

In between the two truths she feels literally pulled, each arm extended and pinned at the palm.

With the friends she attempts a bridging. But instead of ex-plaining with tenderness how it is that she identifies with the anger and defensiveness that lives like the bad child inside her lover, she offers to explain her current physical conditions. This goes badly and makes her sound as if she is hiding her lover behind her own body. She begins with the way her heart is engorged. Why, her heart is only working for her own body at about forty percent. All the rest goes to the growing life. So that her blood isn't even reaching her. She tires easily and feels dizzy all of the time. She then goes into a long description of the way the weight is so concen-trated that it throws off her center of gravity, this too leads to severe fatigue. She makes a noble effort to produce the ar-gument that she is actually doing extraordinarily well for a woman as far along as she is. She quickly moves to a de-scription of her stomach and intestines, how they are all shoved up against her ribs and vertebrae, how eating is ex-treme. How if only she could share a bottle of wine with them all, things would not be so tense. (This is of course true. All perfectly true. Except that the friends are gay, and they have their heads together tilted slightly in their listen-ing, as if to say, what, what, what is that you are talking about?) The friends grow suspicious as animals low to the ground.

With her lover she is equally stupid. She tries to explain that
the friends are misinterpreting his silences. His moods. This
goes horridly. His defensiveness mounts to cinematic proportions, and more and more bile comes out about the
friends, as if they have anything to do with anything (She
knows much of what he is saying is actually not about the
friends at all. She is acutely aware of how the rot that lives
underneath the ground of two people in love sifts up to the
surface, emerges, lives with love as if the maggots and stench
are necessary for organic growth. She understands what an
easy target the friends make and how she is the one at fault
for producing them so easily for sacrifice), as if they are the
heart of the matter.

7. He says: "You take everything good and ruin it because
you are too negative." (This is not only untrue, it is hugely
ironic, which makes tremendous sense to her. She has always
drawn deep irony from people. What is more true is that it is
he who has the difficulty seeing the beauty in things, that he
has told her again and again how she has saved him with the
light that lives inside of her. But it does not matter whether or
not the statement is true about him or true about her. What
matters is that the irony is present between them like a thick
membrane. What matters is that the sentence has haunted his
life or being and that the sentence has haunted her life and
being and the sentence won't die. It keeps getting born.)
Later, after the talking has turned back into their mouths on
one another's flesh, as he is holding her cradled in his arms,
he looks down into her face so near sleep and love or death
and accidentally stumbles upon a sentence that is true
enough—that her sadness is equaled in intensity only by her
ability to feel joy. She thinks it takes the one to feel the other.

8. The next day she watches a too ripe persimmon blow
violently off of the tree outside the window and smash

against a 2000 year old Etruscan wall. One would think
that this would make a symbol for her, an unbearable image overtaking all other meanings. But something has happened underneath the skin of things. Something that is
difficult to see. She has a lesion. It is not so important, this
wounding. And then suddenly it is. She is filled with a
foreign ecstasy. On the one hand it is terrible. A new worry
and complication late in the pregnancy. On the other hand,
it joins them in the flesh, in wounding, in meaning. The
timing of the lesion seems larger than their own lives. A
scene of wounding in this country made of madonnas and
infants. The splitting open of red skin to pulp and seed,
the birds have been waiting, the ground is ready in its
dormancy to hold the cold fruit until it is brought to life by
the sun.

Her sadness which is also joy brings no tears this time, ironi-
cally. They are alone in the house. They are watching the
sky change hues in front of them, like some time-lapse photography, history, belief. Neither speaks for a long while.
She can feel his heart beating inside his body. Finally he
says: "I feel free here. I feel as if a great burden has been
lifted. I love you." She does not feel free, but she remembers
what he is talking about. To be released from one kind of
life into another, to let go the old angers and tortures through
a series of rewritings, to trust that someone will let you, will
wait for you, will ignore the meanings of words and meet
you at the cusp of things again.

She knows what he means, and is thus happy for him. Or if
not happy, then calm in her melancholy. Her smile thus
appears half-formed, or is it that it is drawn inward into
depths we ordinarily cannot speak, down into the world of
what will rise as their son? Miles.

9. Their lives make a cross. Hers, shooting uncontrollably ever upward, even unto death. His, laterally lining a plane of being. Icon is the word for it but the symbol wrestles away from speech. Hasn't it always?

10. Where will they rest?

Beatings

His face has the look of a boxer's mug, but only in certain light, particularly in winter, when shadows and darks and lights stand out in stark contrast from one another. Only when winter gives way to a single barren tree against an almost white sky, or a boulder shoulders its own outline against snow. His fighter's face emerges or recedes according to the light. So too do his eyes, the cups of fatigue underneath each giving way to the flattened spot just above the nose, the jaw clenching and unclenching itself while eating or fighting or fucking or sleeping. You wonder where you have seen this face before, and then you think, his face echoes movies you can picture, men in movies beating back the world, De Niro in *Raging Bull,* Stallone in *Rocky,* Brando in *On the Waterfront.* At first this seems to be untrue, but the more you watch him move, at night, working out, pushing the body against darkness and winter cold, the more it is true, it is the film of a man and not the man, or it is the man caught on film repeating himself. Any image of a man which is against itself, which you suddenly see is any image of a man.

Outside in the gray he works out. Boxing. Short pulses. He faces off against what is called a body opponent bag. It is in the shape of a man's torso. The man's face has the look of an aggressor. He hits. The blows land in the head, the chest.

In his mind ideas seize, recede, then again raise and rise. Fisted speed dug deep and jab extended until it's shot strung back to the shoulder. His thoughts a neverending drive and end, and end, and end, and end.

Inside of the house where it's light he plays the cello. His hands change shape, like birds moving from the dull land to the winged sky. A metronome marks time with ticks, with rocking, with regular, adjustable intervals. Its measures and rules give meaning, sense, divisions and designs to sound. Unvaryingly regular. His hands cupping the instrument. His fingers carrying the crouch of a dream in which chaos orders and slows and sings. The strings as thick as the bones of a hand. The sound reverb bellows up through his wrists, up his forearms, through the shoulders, into the spine.

In winter even the trees are beaten. Gray of asphalt to gray of fence post to gray of field of dormant growings. Gray of the tips of branches and trunks, gray of the hills' hues dulling over, gray of the edges of things against the gray-white sky. Like color is bruised, bludgeoned, deadened.

Up close fingers fingering the thick strings of a cello look like they are something out of a dream. Close up. Suddenly the knuckles are fluid and seemingly without joints. The fingertips ride hard and wide; they tremble then go taut. The white skin stretching between fingers seems more like an infant's than a man's. And when the strings pulse and reverb, it is as if the instrument is of the body and not a wooden hulled-out object. Between his legs its singing rises. From his spine the chords pull up and out. Against his chest the neck presses; even his teeth resonate. The wood grain as deeply brown as his eyes. The notes rebody a body. You must close your eyes.

Any cadence saves him. For what is a cadence but a balanced rhythmic flow, as in poetry, as in the measured beat of movement, as in dancing, as in the rising and falling of music, of the inflections of a voice, modulations and progressions of chords, moving, moving through a point beyond sight, sound, vision, being. To fall, in winter, without ending.

He is thirty. One night he gets up to pee, then crashes dead weight to the floor in the bathroom. His wife finds him. He is having a seizure. He is not conscious. His eyes are open. She lifts his feet slightly even in her fear; blood transfusion. Then she holds his head in her lap and says his name and says his name and says his name until his eyes flutter open, like a fighter coming to. That's how his life became this fight. That's how his fighting became him. When you watch him work out you see a classic Hollywood theme taking form: the Fighter. His fight is with his father. His fight is with himself. His fighting so familiar he cannot recognize it, like a face in the mirror after shocking news.

Behind the fight there is always a woman. His wife. What is her part? She is thinking of all the men in her life. Her father, heart disease. Her first husband, heart murmur. Her second husband, liver and heart disease. Her second husband's father, heart attack. Her first husband's father, heart failure. Her father's father, heart attack. She is thinking she has seen this movie before. She is thinking that a movie today must take what has been told a thousand times and give it a form no one was expecting. This is how she keeps from killing herself.

She is a decade older than he is. She had thought herself to be the one closer to the edge of living. She had thought herself closer to genetic undoing. But it is now that she sees the death in all of us. The heart disease. What she has begun to see is that we are all an audience watching the image of a man fighting. What she has begun to learn is the black and white of slow motion. If she stands at the window and watches him working out, what she sees is a frame at a time. One move following another. The fist pulled back to the shoulder or launched to the false body in separate movements.

Zocor decreases triglyceride levels. Aspirin thins the blood. Fish oil capsules and flax seed oil wage enzyme war against the body's fatty walls. Arteries and blood roads and blued vessels bulge and thin in heavy rhythms. A glass of wine each night transforms from pleasure to prescription. Red meat is torn from animal, instinctual longing, and replaced with white rice, broiled fish, food for the hairless and light bodies of Asian men. He obeys the regimen. He fears the weakness which may attack his bulk. He cannot picture himself; he is afraid he is changing in ways that he cannot live with.

He decides that he will begin to film himself working out and playing cello. First he doesn't know why. Later he decides that the films will be for his son.

No one's home movies are black and white. All of them by now have that eerie super-eight technicolor blur haze, its hues dulling reality into frames and shutter speed. He has no home movies. He never knew his father. The films he makes are in black and white. The rushes hang in strips down the wall of the door to the bathroom, or coiled onto white reels like little wheels. He tells himself he and his son will watch them together. He the fatherless. The images living and turning forever. Like a private movie star. Like old movies of prize fighters. Remember that the last

scenes determine whether or not you will see the film again.
And again.

She watches him work out. She admires the violence with
which he fights. She thinks that if the body opponent bag
were alive, he would kill it. She smiles. She smiles because
they both believe in film.

We believe in the fighting. Still. We want to see the raging
bull, a boxer beaten by a tragic flaw. We want to cheer for
Rocky, we want to see a man's love bringing his violence to
life—his fighting saving him and providing the happy ending necessary for sequel upon sequel. We want to see a
fighter who is forced into labor that is not his die a heroic
death. We want to see his own integrity kill him. We want
Brando. We do not want the movie of a man who is losing
heart.

Aikido, karate, judo, tae kwon do, arts of combat, of beauty,
of sport, of self defense, of speed and thought, of the body
unbodied from its tasks of being and let loose into movement and rhythm, of the arms unarming themselves, the
wrists cocked back to fluid animal past rotations, the shoulders dipping and curling, of the neck forgiven its upright
burden and relearning the side to side and back and under
tricks of instinct, of the chest and biceps pumping and bulg-
ing like meated masses, of the hands letting go of tools and
becoming not a part of the body, but the body itself, of all of
the internal organs in symphony and not against one another, not individuated, but of one measured movement after another, as if the entire corpus was what drove things,
and not the heart alone.

He doesn't know it but his numbers are improving, the good
cholesterol beating the bad, the fats fading in sebaceous

white waves. He doesn't see it but his weight is dropping, muscle, spine and nerve replacing the soft buffer which had been between the world and his heart. For isn't it his father's body he has inherited? He doesn't feel it but his heart's beating is no longer against him, though he fights as if everything, even the moon, were against him. Still, inside of his body, invisible, his heart is finding a rhythm which will bring him life, calm, like the soft pink of an open palm.

What is it? What was it? His father dead at thirty-three. Heart attack. The blood blocked, the oxygen cut off. The muscle, that fist-shaped meat, unable to breathe. His father. Thirty-three. Heart attack. Words like thrusts. And all that living up and through him. What is it? What is it? What? His fists asking.

He is working out in front of the house. His fist connects whap smack solid with his body opponent bag. He catches a glimpse in his peripheral vision of his wife and son inside the house, as if the house is a body, his wife and son a heart, watching, beating, smelling like infant's skin and milk. Then he strikes a blow straight to the chest of the false body. It is a kind of hope, this beating.

Siberia: Still Life of a Moving Image

I. Phosphorescence

There is a photo in the palm of her hand.

Her mouth is not visible.

Her face lost to his.

She does not know what day it is and she knows what day it is precisely. White cotton and white lace and white linen and layers of girl. She is a child in the photo. No. Not a child. A girl moving toward woman in the strangest of days, a day where all the light is cold, white on white, out of time.

He has taken a black and white photograph of her in a field of buttercups the spring before this cold. Though he doesn't know it, he will carry the photo with him in black and white and gray against his heart. He will dream the yellow of the field as her hair. He will dream the white of her skirts as snow in a forest. His camera, small friend, confidant, prayer. The frame around the girl is the box of his entire world. He does not even know the language of love, only small bumbling nudges that his adolescent body makes around the edges of tables, the frames of doors, a knee at a desk finding its bruise, feet that break walking again and again.

It is as if love were ever this simple.

It is as in a small room of a house, people make their lives inside, stories, images, breath. It is as in a house empty of its inhabitants. One day he brings the photo to the girl and holds it between them as another palm. Almost as soft as a whisper she takes it between her hands or holds it to her face (strange…had she thought it was another face? One better or stronger than her own?) or puts her tongue to it. She does not know; he doesn't either. It is as if a rush of blood drives her body to lunge at him, to knock him all the way to falling to the floor.

She smiles; her mouth opens more slightly than molecules of air slipping across flesh. Their bodies move into one another; centrifugal force. His hands fold and fold into folds of white and find her hot and wet and flesh that is not flesh but the heart exploded inside out to soft tenderness. His hands have no idea. She is ripping the bodice apart as plucking the feathers from fowl; rage or something. They have no idea. His ache hard his rising at the hips her falling or opening or they don't know what.

Her face: kissed with blood. His: glistening.

In this spring there has been no war for years. It is as if war has left the frame of the world. It is as if the days will bring bodies to light, as if the nights will surrender to touch and tune, heat coming inexplicably.

2. Camera Obscura

In the prison he is visited by his wife every month. She brings him a little wooden box with some food and a letter hidden between bottom boards. He hides the letters in the box underneath the planks on the floor.

For five years he keeps himself alive by reading letters and staring at a single photograph.

After five years his mind, he finds, wanders in ways that are closer to DNA, the movement of the stars, blood driven by biology.

One night, for example, he wakes thinking about a young man he met from the university. The young man had told him about how professors and students were either in prison or no longer among the living. He had related the story with such great sadness, even though he and his family were of the elite. He had thought at the time, that is a great generosity of feeling; these young men ordinarily have no reverence for history or the great tragedies of culture. He had thought, these young men will one day grow out of prisons and toward some other world, perhaps the world of art; this is at least what he hoped for the young man, who spoke at times of literature with tremendous intimacy. The young man described how the language of lectures had dropped from intellectual to ideologically banal or militaristic, and how that disappointed him. What struck him most, and the thought that invaded his current mind-state, was the way that the young man had spoken again and again of the beauty of the library and the even more beautiful courtyards. And he found himself thinking without permission and certainly without deference to his current situation, which was, of course, beyond grave, that what the boy had been taken with was the architecture of place, which was, in his opinion, the same thing that moved him toward photography. That what he had been after with his little lens and mechanical box was the attempt to frame the architecture of place, its aura, its fleeting and untraceable "ness."

This thought then brought him to the last photo he had taken of his wife, standing in a field of buttercups next to a river, an image he would for some terrible reason unknown to him lose in his fifth year of prison, and then to the last two photos he had taken before he had been arrested: one of the massacre, the other of a gutted corpse in the foreground and a dead, decomposing horse in the background. The face of his wife, the murders, the corpses; each a precise architecture of place, like a building creating form from chaos, like a city emerging from bombed out rubble and decay.

Then the memory of the young man fades and never returns, as if it had never existed.

After five years he began to have nightmares: a bloody torso inching its way along the frozen ground, a leg without a body being pulled by a dead horse. He wakes in the night as if waking were sleeping and sleeping labor. A few days ago he met a man from a town he perhaps knew in his previous life. The man had stolen wood and was awaiting sentencing. Two days ago they had taken the man away. Yesterday he had returned. They had cut off one of his legs as punishment. He remembered thinking that a man's leg looked a great deal like an enormous stick of bread. They brought it back with them and threw it out where it could be seen from the barracks. Each day corpses were piled onto sleighs and prisoners harnessed like horses would pull them with ropes, drag them several hundred meters from the barracks and pile them up as if for a bonfire. But never the leg. He thought the image of a corpse's hair or skin frozen to the sleigh's wood, peeling off the skull or the face was the more horrific. But the leg. Left to rot there in front of them but not, freezing instead, not decomposing as an ordinary leg might. It is strange what moves us and what does not.

Many bodies in the barracks would rest for days dead next to sons or daughters too weak to lift them. These would be dragged out by ropes into the pile.

And then his thoughts would fragment and tumble again. A common treatment for frostbite was to hang a body, barely living, from the ceiling. One girl with sores all over her was hung by the armpits. One man so starved and shrunken as to appear to be a boy was hung by his feet. He died within hours.

Men would come and go either in his mind's eye or in real time. One was a writer. With this man there was almost a joy, although secret and pinched, small and guilt-stricken, that lived while they were dying together. It sat like a rock between their dissolving bodies. He without a camera and he without any means of recording his thoughts on paper.

If he could produce a picture he would produce one of the human body lost to death but living like words. A frozen image. Hundreds of people curled fetal in their bunks like strange snails because scurvy had infected their joints. The worst of these were bodies in heaps and strange little piles indistinguishable from clods of dirt and rags and their own defecations. The white nights blew beyond thought and cracked the bone with a cold previously unimagined. People had reached the point that they had no sex, just the vague skeletal cage of a body, mouths sunken in from lost teeth and disease, eyes glassy and hollowed out holes. Their tailbones protruded, taking them back to their animal past.

He and the writer spoke many times of the ice graves that housed them. White and more white and ceilings of ice, walls of ice, floors of ice. Not a building at all, the space around what should have been the building invaded it and lived there without proper form. A space fifty centimeters wide allotted for each person. No roofs or walls, just planks standing in place of architecture. He described to the writer a photo he had taken of a gardening tool frozen in ice. He had thought at the time that it was a very metaphoric image, of time, of age and youth. Together they spoke of the terrible loss of that image, how it would be lost to them forever, how the metaphor was dead, no photo or poem could liberate it from this decay. And they had agreed, as they agreed to stop eating the too salty herrings that produced such enormous thirst as to drive the body to drinking urine, as they had vowed to suffer hunger with the conviction and steadfastness of someone choosing to fight for their country, they agreed between them like the small stone that was their hearts but had long since petrified that they would choose starvation as being.

One day the writer was taken away, and he did not see him again. His strength faltered, as with the loss of a lover or wife, as when the blood or love leaves the body. He thought he saw him several times, far in the distance, in the night, the moon shining over a frozen forever in endless horizons. He would peer out from sleeplessness and in a delirium of cold, and he thought he could see the writer framed by sky and the white of snow, the writer as a skeletal figure, harnessed like a horse, dragging the leg, with…was it buttercups? Buttercups falling from the sky…all the images of his life blurring into one.

Did he forget himself? He finds himself standing exposed,
as if shitting in a field in the hours of a long day's labor, his
genitals slowly sucking back into the cavities of the body,
shrinking, retreating back. The cold. He is squatting, vulgar.
He has no idea how long he has been this way. In sight the
others are gathering wood, thistles, cones from a forest. A
guard with a rifle and with a cigarette for a mouth. The rifle
is at rest less than five feet from his own skull. What a camera would make, in the middle of nowhere, not human but
characters of human, garish colors against the starkest of
white. He thinks he sees a flash of red. A woman leaning in
to kiss the face of a lascivious soldier; no. A German shep-
herd dog's tongue too pink against snow, licking a palm. A
man's penis against snow.

He redresses. Trousers in threads pulled up as if they are
pants, as if they covered a body. He looks out across white
and on the white peopled spots of black and gray and the
hint of flesh. Faces? Holes for eyes and mouths. Is it a crowd?

A crowd not unlike in a city, normal, in flux, the arcades
beckon, the people move or arrest, now drawn into the call
of a vendor, meat, or liquor, warmth, the kindness of the
exchange, ordinary goods and services, from one hand to the
next, one body to the next, words traded kindly about the
afternoon and the trade and the hands, the faces giving and
receiving, the light of an afternoon. Sensory perceptions.

Broken into white, black lifeless twigs moving in obscene
jerking tilts. Arms retrieve sticks from fallen trees. Legs barely
able to carry a body pushing through blankets of white as if
slow motion or a broken film. As if the entire photo were
overexposed, the humans faint impressions of themselves.

He opens his mouth as if it is a shutter. The speed is with
him. He is a machine, he is a small box capturing light and
movement into stasis. He is clicking as blinking, he is uttering a single word. "Tiesa." The guard cocks a trigger in a

perfectly synchronous motion. He is moved through sound
to join the stick-like figures nearly cracking from the trick of
their actions. He is now part of the scene.

Already he has nostalgia for the friend who died into
white, into a frozen object left inanimate and stunned. He
remembers washing the man's back. The rag following the
moles of his back as if they made some strange constellation, his own hand magnified to him, more than human, the
man's flesh taking the hand's motions as a gentle whisper,
red where he rubbed, and then vanishing into steam. Dirt
and disease erased in small circles underneath the picture of
his hand. The man's nape bent away from him, the limb of
a tree, or the arc of metal, the rough tendrils of black hair
barely visible, the head so forward. The giving over to love,
the tiniest of gestures exploding like bombs. And what was
in his eyes as he gazed upon a man's back? Did he look
upon the back with longing? Where were the definitions of
words going? How is it that he is haunted by the parts of a
body? The leg, the torso, the tenderness of the curves, and
valleys of a spine? The black curls of the back of his head,
so black, so coarse, so like a forest he wanted to rest his face
there, calmly and without intention, as natural as putting a
head to a pillow or to the breast of a woman? Why the pull
to mouth the vertebrae, one at a time, with patience? Why
the magnetic pull to put his arms around the faceless torso,
to wrap his legs around legs from behind, yes, to say the
sentence, I would like to rest my face in your hair, I would
like to lean my body into yours, can you support my weight,
even for ten seconds, will you pull back, will we remember
our former selves?

And cupping his own elbows in the alone. And rocking
his own sad form against the night. And muscles unknown
to him, begging touch. And his head, too heavy, lolling to
the side, eyes rolling back into memory, throat dry and bone
white and teeth unnatural ache and fists clenching and

unclenching. Oh to let go into death. To follow him, as a slave or a lover, into death, into the white wanting, into the image neverending. The body dissolving. The light an accident, making photography of their lives.

Father?

In his tenth year he is scratching his name into wood. An elderly man, emaciated but for his rotund and hard as a melon belly, laughs out loud, a thunderous laugh, almost hideous. The man cannot stop. He gives his best to ignore him, continues an attempt to remember the letters of his own name, the year, the day. Finally he turns to the cackling nightmare of a man and tells him to go fuck himself. It is the first time he has used obscenity in that way for years. What would be the point? Anger is a luxury. The man, now weeping from laughter, finally subsides, a few chortles and snorts linger; he sits on a piece of wall jutting away from the rest. He wipes his eyes with rags, clothing.

My dearest friend, please, I beg of you, forgive my intrusion. As it happens, I was just thinking to myself that all my life has been given over to an insanity. You will wonder what I mean. In my case it was science. I have, as I say, given my life to the study of science, if you can believe that, the pursuit of that brand of knowledge in which the proven outscores the given. And at the age of seventy, as least I think that is the age, and in my nineteenth year here, at least that is what I have tallied, given number to, it happened into my mind that the waste has not been these years in prison, but rather the years I spent toiling away in my lab, working for the state, believing with all my heart as I did that physics was beyond anything, beyond patriotism or god, beyond the heart, the head, the concerns of the body, beyond any thought or drive. I thought then something like, "I am giving my life to the magnificent order of the universe freely and with zealousness." And when I saw you sitting there, friend, and please believe my apology sincere, I meant no harm nor disrespect, when I saw you sitting there with your little scrap of metal trying to record a name, was it a name? Was it your name? No matter; when I saw you, it reminded me of all my righteous planning and sacrifice to the tiny world of microscopic and mathematical pinpoints. Do you see?

In the time that he knew the old man it seemed to him that there was not a single moment in which he was not talking. Not narrating his knowledge even in the face of its destruction and uselessness. It was as if an entire human history were pouring forth from his mouth in little bodies and words, calmly and without desperation, an even tone, and on, on. He believed himself to be dying in fact, a cancer, yes, he was certain, his great and authentic big-headed knowledge of science assured him like second sight, so he thought, that his body was indeed being invaded, bombed, taken over, so to speak. Whether or not the man was correct he hadn't a clue. The man's face was reddened always, but other than that, he never noticed anything out of the ordinary in all the speeches, the conversations, musings, unending philosophies forming small orbits and universes out there against the white. He only knew that he wished the old man would go on speaking forever, since he had discovered that his primary fear, the one he had been plagued with and tormented by, believing himself to be more of a coward than any other prisoner could possibly be, was that he was losing his aesthetic, and thus his ability to see pictures and chart the world in his way. He thought that listening to the old man in a way imprinted where his brain was dissolving, because it was sure enough that the old man was an intellect of the traditional and perhaps by now dead and gone variety, of the type the world was losing to machines and ideologies, even before the wars.

But in between the scrolls of history and knowledge and information spilling over his lips there in the barren and iced existence they shared came small mythologies or fairy tales, little details barely audible, sometimes recited as the old man was drifting off to sleep toward morning, sometimes in between some arduous journey through a mathematical equation that the old man was attempting to render in the form of a visual image, sometimes in ordinary conversation, pointing to something invisible there in the distance, as if he were pointing at the very edge of the imagination, a horizonless place where words proved sight wrong and ideas formed like trees just out of the corner of an eye.

The day of their liberation, after they had forgotten their own names, officers began shooting prisoners at random, even as the officers were themselves fleeing in jeeps, even as they were being overrun by troops, their quarters burned to the ground, their leaders handcuffed and scorned and whisked away for war crimes or picked up off of the ground after suicides, still, the soldiers were shooting prisoners as best they could, and the old man went on talking, a bullet to the head as he headed for the truck, a photographer's hand held out to him with a few fingers still tingling with life, the old man babbling away, storming from the mouth with the last vestiges of history, saying something, what was it, something about Galileo, and wasn't that extraordinary, that he looked into the night sky and reversed an entire epoch, wasn't it though, who among us would ever raise their head to a night sky like that again? And his head rocked back with the shot and his mouth red agape as if endlessly laughing, toward a dead heaven, toward a godless sky, into the white.

3. Lens

She appeared as if a whisper, digging potatoes with a spade. The hands of a child. No. Not a child. A tiny woman already grown, already unable to claim the face of innocence. The small body of too much knowing. Her hands: furious. Her little feet wrapped and wrapped with rags and shoved down into shoes not hers. Her furious digging.

I call out to her. She is startled, holds the spade as a weapon for an instant, then lowers her hand to nothing. But her eyes hold me there in the cold afternoon, two eyes staring into two eyes, we are making statues, we are trying to understand the outlines of two lives, a woman and a girl, we are trying to remember what strangers do for one another out of hiding, out of fear, out of the long wait waiting. Is it spring? No. It is the end of winter, but not spring.

Each day I begin the page the same. What is it to lose love. And each day I look at the sentence and understand completely the overbearing pathos, the cliché. I am thinking of the way sentences die, or the way someone dies and a sentence cannot hold the weight, of the way language gives way again and again, despite our dreadful longing to *get it right*. There is no getting it right. I have seen many losses, grief, a woman or a man unable to bear what is gone. They find themselves in the world as strange white birds, their hands transformed into wings, unable to hold anything. They flutter about trying to grab at objects or people, but as we know from observing a dog or a cat they cannot *hold*. And thus their wingedness gives them empty hands, or the impossibility of hands. This is loss: the impossibility of hands.

The truth is I am uniquely suited for loss. I know from the start that I am better able to cope than most. Like Medusa, knowing her fate before her death. I will not, for instance, suicide. And I will not starve myself, nor drool into madness. In a way that makes the pain more stark, more outlined, more complete. I am so close to naming it, even as language fails. I am certain my love could have photographed it, and I know artists who could have painted it, artists burned alive because they could see, all of us could name, whether by image or word. This is not new. It has happened for ages and thus has no weight except in repetition. A poem. Perhaps this is why poetry stuns us so.

I am uniquely suited. My body is not small and frail as a woman's, but sturdy and thick as a peasant's. My jaw stern and my hands strong. My breasts full but not with milk or motherhood. My calves two large fruits, my feet flat to the ground. Only a certain kind of man would love this version of a woman. In her he would see strength giving over to a child, the way a child experiences wonder and, in the next moment, smashes the head of an animal—a snake, a frog—with pure joy. Or the way a child dismembers an insect, or spends an entire day building a small city out of blocks only to smash it to pieces with the same hands. How godlike. The child's changing loyalties, enemies suddenly perfect in their fascination, loved ones thrown over like limp corpses into a fire. A man would have to be able to see this. He must want to touch it. He must understand that the world's visions of women hold no answers, that they steal away in the night, leave a body as if dehydrated. He must want the palms of his hands around something immovable and mutable at the same instant. He must be unafraid of this and yet terrified. He must understand life in death, stasis in movement, the heat of passion in shredding flesh to bits.

I am not broken. But I am circular in my thinking; perhaps this is what it is to be mad with loss. The things I write hold no sense or tune. I wrote just now of men and women, of a certain kind of love, and I have not the faintest idea of what I am saying. It is at moments such as this that I believe with every molecule of existence, with all the ridiculous folds of the brain, that language is a parlor trick, a trompe l'oeille that makes us risk lived experience for imagination. To think that a word could hold anything on its small back. What a farce. What a cruel joke. I am an idiot and my hands are addicted.

I leave her there. I go back into the house. She continues her digging, watchful but concentrated on the task. It is ordinary for us to ignore one another.

I find her asleep in the shed that night, buried under straw and wood. I find her there again in the morning. We do nothing to care about one another. This happens for days. Perhaps a week. I do not care how many days, and she is making a life utterly without me, there in the shed at night, out in the yard by day, eating potatoes or roots or whatever it is that is keeping her alive.

Is it fatigue that moves us this way? To keep our distance? Or is it simply that it hurts too much to care for another human? We speak of the human spirit, how it holds up, how triumphant, graceful, heroic. But in the end thousands have ignored one another so that we might return to our ordinary boredoms in peace. So that we did not suicide. After great movements to save one another our surrender came as the body reclaiming itself, a simple thought: I want to go home, I want the quiet of the room of a house, I do not want to struggle to survive by building small communities. I want to die in my house, alone, the sight of all my memory a tiny picture inside a thick skull.

It is not that I want her to die. It is simply that I do not want to care about her life.

She is brilliant in her reciprocity. She never comes to the door of the house, she never asks for anything. And I think, a person could live their entire life in these terms. Not a mother. Not a daughter.

One day I fall from the roof. I had been there to patch a leaking space, and cold and tired and not paying attention, I fell. She only stopped to look for an instant, pausing inside her world, turning her little face toward my falling, my body dumb and large on the hard ground, the end of winter, a woman she does not know. Something is wrong with my back, but not terribly so. I can get up. I can make it back into the house. At the door I pause; holding myself up I look back at her. She does not move. She is more still than is humanly possible. Like a photo.

Inside the rooms of my house I search and dig and ache to unbury a single photo from a box, my hands fluttering through the small squares, myself as a girl. Blonde hair. Digging in dirt.

The next day I do not even get out of bed.

The next day I bring her a jar of water, one half of a cabbage, sugar. I place them in a wooden box with the photograph outside the door of the shed before she wakes. You will think I wanted to take care of her. But it is not this. Her indifference moved me. The stillness of watching my injury, the disaffected face, the little hands undeterred.

The next day I write.

4. Emulsion

Alise Tapinitc has no history. Long behind her like small rows of blue corn flowers shivering in the wind. A faded and wrinkled piece of a photograph inside her shirt, next to her skin: family. A father, a mother. Brother. Her understanding of death. Death is a family, death is this wandering from farm house to farm house until a stranger makes it impossible to stay.

Alise Tapinitc has chosen this place randomly. Inside the window in night an image of a woman bent over a desk. Writing. Like the image in her head of her father, drawing and drawing. The hint of a remembered past in the image of a figure bent over paper, pen in hand, intense scrutiny of a white page, the head crooked forward like the angle of a street lamp, eyes weary and set deep into folds and lines of flesh, the light in the room. The curve of the spine. Love.

Alise Tapinitc holds a spade from memory. In that place there was a vegetable garden, a garden with a mother and all their hands and fingers fluttering in the dirt.

This is such a field, though dead and unattended for who knows how long. This is such a figure, a house not a home but the ghost of one. Alise Tapinitc believes she could stay

here for a long while. The cold is leaving; warmth brushes
in like whisper.

A far away vision, the ruins of a church. Or was it some
other place? A central building, a post, a bank, a town hall?
She has no idea. But cathedral centers in her mind as a
drawing from her father. Charcoal and with imprecise lines.
Still the vision. Across the field it rises in jagged lines and
pushes up toward sky irreverent as stone. *Like the heart.*
This is the heart moving toward heaven, not knowing it is
only sky. This is all our hope surging up toward the blue-gray
sky, deep in wonder, lost in wishing. We think there is a per-
fect family there, glistening with white. We want there to be a
son, a mother. The father designs. The daughter is lost, un-
available to the story, hovering like an angel, or is it an idea,
floating in the sky just above our heads?

One would not know this, even watching, but Alise
Tapinitc is building a small city in the mud and rocks and
thistles. One might think that she is digging and digging for
survival, for potatoes, roots, edible ground. However, in her
mind she sees an entire city that she will rebuild in every
field of her life. A small mound here for the center of things,
a cathedral, a butcher's, a factory where paper is made, a
small store for ink and paint and pencils thick as a finger.
Charcoal in thin wafer-like lengths or like a thumb. Oils.
People as small bits of grass, twigs, little stones. Lining the
streets. For trees, pieces off of the ends of trees. For walls,
shale set upon its side. For the hills just outside of the town,
mounds of mud. For the streets, pebble to pebble. For the
sun, hay wrapped and wrapped into a misshapen ball, set
upon a hill, endless setting or rising.

It is a child's game, to build a city over and over like that.

The day she sees the woman fall from the roof she has
finished the tiny city. Its inhabitants look up, remarking,
"Look, the sun is setting on this beautiful day, god and his
family are resting and smiling." But Alise Tapinitc knows

that the people are of her own making, their hope constructed, their existence the imagination of a girl wandering.
Dirt. Weeds. Sticks. Still, she does not think of them as stupid or without understanding. She thinks: *We all choose our
visions, our designs.* The day she sees the woman fall from
the roof she thinks: *This is an interruption, a great cosmic
event. Like blood in the veins, a river winding its way through
a body, a story begging fields and furrows in land.* The ground
shook a bit, a thud of sorts, she had not even realized the
woman was there. She turned her head as slight as the sun
folding behind a cloud, momentarily. The woman did not
look at her immediately. In the time that the woman did not
look at her ideas formed in her head, pictures from everywhere. A boat sliding into a harbor, its red masts and the
white hull and a name in black on the side: Rosemonde.
The side of her father's face bent toward his hands in the
stillness of a candle's flame, its wavering caught for an instant as if in a box of sight. Her brother a dot long off in a
field, pinwheels for arms; no. He is swinging great sticks
that extend his human arms into god-like wings; no. He is
carrying fish on a pole, caught that day in the river. The
bank of the river, small stones pathing down to water, her
magnified feet, waiting. A fire. No, a loud crash. Not that
either. A bomb that envelops everything you thought was
your life.

It is nothing.

By the time Alise Tapinitc's eyes raise to the woman's her
head is lost in some other world where a family disinte-
grates into ash and color. Their eyes meet. Alise Tapinitc
thinks: *it is nothing.* She turns back to her city of dirt and
her hands, caked with mud, resign themselves to their building. There is but one thing left to build, and that is nearly
unimaginable. She must build a river by cupping her hands
and scooping away a path down the center of the city, then
fill it with water (though she has yet to discover water in this

place; she has not searched for a well, a river or lake, a hole of mud), then place the smallest of leaves into its stream. Boats. A city without boats has no blood.

There is a small photo that lives between her ear and her jaw. It is a photo that Alise Tapinitc sees often. It is of an ordinary nature to her, routine, as a baker's truck delivering bread, or a woman carrying her great bags of groceries from the market to the house, along the river front, a dog barking as she passes, a flock of birds lifting to the sky as hands in prayer. It is herds of soldiers the colors of stone or wall lifting from stone or wall as drawings taking on life into marching and the click of boots and heels. It is the gray-green of uniforms moving in unity erasing human as if human were a smudge on a perfect black and white page. It is legs gone beyond walking into a forced trudge that remakes the world. It is the faces of men passing by in huge rows and rows the flesh changed in color and texture to some ceramic thick ball turned to the side atop shoulders then ahead the eyes black. It is bodies bludgeoned and the splatter of red onto the gray-green arms onto the stones of the gray street onto the gray walls it is the bodies going limp as a fish brought to shore thunked in the head and rendered lifeless and dropped into the pile of the day's catch it is the almost eyes from behind windows or doors not there and yet witnessing, it is the light—not night and not day, and in between, not horror nor joy, ordinary, the marks of a passing day in a city. It is a mother and a father and a brother fading from color to gray.

5. Resolve

As the woman lifts herself from the ground, Alise Tapinitc's hands rest upon her knees, she is in a squat, the squat of a child. The woman looks over at Alise Tapinitc and thinks: *My god*. The woman is in love, having witnessed an emotionless face, a naked head with black eyes, hands resting in the middle of some crushing motion. She had always suspected the violence of children. She had never longed to cradle a baby in her arms, feel its warm spit and tongue and mewing mouth at her breast. But this. This raw face glaring at her. How could a woman resist the passion of it? Her entire body quivering heat. Her arms finding themselves. Whatever had fractured or broken losing its weight in her mind. Pushing herself from hand to wrist to forearm to shoulder, lifting her own body, whatever it was, up toward a standing belief, heaving toward the door. The child unmoving. Exquisite. Her arm against the door frame. The child still watching but unmoved. Her hands, still. Her face, still. The pain rising in the base of the woman's spine, in her left hip, shot of electricity up her left side, threading through her vertebrae, into the neck and jaw. Her left eye twitching in a hint of communication, then dropping closed as her head hangs.

When the woman opens her eyes again and lifts her head
the child's watching is gone, gone as the crowds of people
who made up her life in this town, gone as the buildings
that spoke to the land, gone as the fields yielding fruit and
feed and the animals grazing and your feet in the tall grass
or the ice of the river. An ending making itself present. Her
love for this child is tremendous, as a lover taken into the
cunt of a woman, as arms encircling the torso or hips, pulling the grinding closer, taking the smell of sweat in, mouths
engulfing mouths, as a body tensing up toward a body, receiving, or is it giving, life?

No one is looking. A woman and a child at the end of a
winter.

Their crossing happens in an instant, without background
or context, and without a future. There is a rainstorm. The
woman comes from the inside of the house and begins to
scoop away at the earth to form a kind of irrigation away
from the house, so that the water will not enter, so that a
small stream will carry the weight of the sky around her life.
The girl emerges from the shed like a small rodent, her eyes
fixed and her face concentrated on the hands, the arms, the
arched back and brow of the woman. She gathers stones
from the field and carries them two at a time to make a kind
of tiny wall in the places where the ditch needs reinforce-
ment. Nothing is at stake, to be flat, however, the integrity of
the gestures seems to rise above the flatness like a sentence
or chorus, the beginning of a line, the image moving toward
art. And so it is in this way that now and again their hands
touch, though they never look at one another, and now and
again their shoulders brush, as two bodies crouching again
and again in the direction of the ground might, by chance,
with nothing communicated. Branches in the wind, a curl of
water around a rock.

When they are finished they stand drenched and covered
in mud from hand to forearm, hair like seaweed or birds'

nests, each gazing out in the direction of the stream of their design, water moving away from the house.

Inside the house the woman heats lemon water. The girl seats herself by a fire dwindling; her hands resuscitate the flames. Neither speaks. There is hard bread and cheese. There is meat as well, eaten silently.

More water is heated in a large tin tub. Not large enough for a body, unless it is the body of a child. The woman washes herself with a rag. When she is finished, she moves away to a corner, sits in a chair, closes her eyes, puts her hand to her face. The girl removes her clothing from the waist up, bends, dips the entirety of her torso, head, face, into the warm water. She holds herself under there. The woman glances at her, then closes her eyes again. When the girl emerges from the water her face is half shining in fire-light, her hair slick as a snail's secretion, her hands moving like a small water creature's might, pruning the face, the ears, the neck. The girl sits there like that in front of the fire, her hands cupping her elbows, her face lost inside itself, not thought, but the body, only the body.

After a time the woman undresses herself to a white faded silk slip and folds herself between white linen sheets and a woolen gray blanket on a wooden bed. The girl does not hesitate. Nor does she consider the gesture, the movement of her own body. Quite simply she crawls into the small of the woman's back, her face nestled against the spine, her breathing, within minutes, matching the rhythm of the body before her. Her fist underneath her chin. The woman, from sleep, feels the tiny trace of butterfly wings at her spine, or the whisper of buttercups falling from the sky, or the heat of a tiny orphaned bird crossing the geography of her back.

Eventually, in the way the sky goes from stark white and bone cold to honey and heat, the woman tells Alise Tapinitc the story of her husband. Alise Tapinitc, in return, describes the pictures in her head that were a family.

Eventually, in the way that time marks the body with lines, bruises, or small discolorations at the hands, face, chest, Alise Tapinitc is sent to America.

6. Representation

This is the story of a woman who is unknown to me. It is the only story I can bring myself to tell. It is a nexus wherein the larger unbearable narrative of things breaks down into bits and pieces like snow or blood.

I have tried to tell the story of myself and I cannot. I work instead from a handful of John's photographs. Echoes of his body, his eyes. One photo in particular ravaged the movements of our lives. It is the beginning and the end, and then again it is neither of these; it is without beginning and I am as if an ending passes through me continuously as water.

September. A large and busy ward filled with wounded soldiers. The army had marched in. The airport had been bombarded. Doctors worked without attention to the hours changing from day to night toward a passage of time marked with red on endless white and sutures that only multiplied and screamed like the mouths of trapped animals.

There was a nurse named Zina. Next to her image John wrote her name.

Zina's body held up with a spine from memory. Her muscles weighted down like ancient lead. Exhaustion familiar. In a single sentence she drew fate to herself. She said,

"Will there ever be an end to all this…how much longer can it last?" When she saw a guard motioning with his crooked finger for her to come to him, a convulsion overtook her body for an instant. Her feet lodged in the ground as if she had been turned to stone. Cold spit lined the inside of her mouth. I did not know her, and yet I know her through lens and light, through a mechanical box.

It is like this. A sentence. An image. Ruin.

These are our times, and yet, were there ever other times, is there a time in some other land where the slight weight of a word or an image does not crush the possibility of the world? In such places, if they do exist, are their corners not raging with murder and despair in some silent pantomime just under the belly of a body making shadow? I cannot unfurl the folds of my brain in the direction of such a place. For if we exist in this time and our audience fails to notice, then is it not possible that we are the imaginary itself? A lack, an absence, a silence. Perhaps I work from John's images because I cannot speak the language of the present.

In the story, Zina immediately rushes to the operating room and begs the surgeons to tell the soldiers that she is needed in the operating room. They are in the middle of an operation. Scalpels unclean but alive carve and slip in and out of bodies, as if the bodies were strange unnamed geography. The speed with which the surgeons work reflects that time has deformed. The heads of the surgeons are bent over meat or land, the hands of the surgeons dip in and out of bodies, saving or killing, is this healing?

The surgeons send for Zina—they want to save a life. After a space the soldiers invade the operating room, and, not finding the nurse, who has leapt like an animal out a window into the night, they convulse into a furious rage. They give an order. She must be found within ten minutes. This order rings in the room, a dead bone echo to bone white wall to bloody apron sunk into frantic imperative. Of course the soldiers return not in ten minutes but before that time. There is no woman found. The two surgeons are ripped from their patient and arrested. A man bleeds to death on a table.

Into the night with surgical gowns billowing like blood-splattered sails and gloves of a butcher and dragged through the streets. The black and wet streets and the dragging of the blood and the gowns and the gloves and the bodies. A third almost random surgeon is added to the terrible parade. He had been sent to find the nurse, but he did not find the woman, and he said, "She is not here," and so was dragged as well. The nurse hears. In a room hidden by strangers she is told, she is consumed with guilt, she gives her body over to the movements of not history, but the creatures that live inside of us. She gives herself up, unable to bear the weight of three men tortured or killed. Unable to bear the weight of three men in a history that will evaporate as quickly as it arrives.

This is happening in the space of one hour.

People not of the streets but behind walls inside doors near windows hear the screams and the cries of the surgeons the martyrs the frozen still shot mouths unable to shut. Four bodies are thrown into a dungeon-like basement. Out of language. Time.

Later, relatives and other nurses come to prepare them for burial. The faces are unrecognizable. Meat or land disfigured. The bodies are identified by small evidence of clothing torn to shreds.

John photographs this massacre. I was with him. What is a body when it is not a body? A face bludgeoned beyond mouth, nose, eyes?

I looked into the faces, but my perception was not that of any reality I knew. To look into an other's face ordinarily gives over a return, a looking back, a second self. I looked into the faces, and only dirt and bile rose up my gullet as if

I had swallowed death whole, as if maggots and rot had eaten me from the inside out and my body was turning, turning from living to dead, from blood driven to corpse. No. Not dead. Unliving. I work from a photo of unliving matter.

John is taken from me later. The photos are evidence. They take nearly all of them.

The first five years I took him a small wooden box with some food and a letter. Every month.

Later I could not get word, nor body, nor any form of longing to my love. I am unburied.

You will wonder why parts of the story are missing. Why I cannot supply the entire history of the massacre. The name of the city. What news was reported. I ask you for patience. I am now speaking a language out of sense. For the first time in nearly fifty years a story was published in the newspaper. This is foreign to you.

I suspect that there are many scratches and as yet unfinished sentences emerging in quiet corners of households, hidden beneath pillows or floorboards, behind stoves or toilets, papers and pages and white or yellowed parchments carrying the black inked story of a husband, a father, of mothers, children. They will all flutter up to the sky someday in their smallness. In their dislocation from history. They will escape like deranged birds, or hands waving insanely in a sky incapable of containing them. Put these with those.

Am I losing my mind? Does the mind let go before the body recognizes it, or is it the other way around? What is this place that I refuse to leave it? What was it, how is it that I became the word of its name? Snow like petals. It is in me or it is me, and I am lost without this land. Did I stay for John? For the image that killed him? Is that my name, in that image of love or atrocity, a photo that I return to as a lover, day, night, month, year, never leaving, never moving?

The word does not know my name, and why should it? A lifetime vigil of remembering, and for what? Larger stories

have consumed the smallness of ours. Look at a map, will
you?

I have learned a great deal about images. It used to be
that an image held a kind of aura. You could hold a photograph in your hands and feel its power. I sound idiotic, I
know. I look at my hands and they remind me of these
pages on which I have written so many words to no one.
Who would take my story into their life? No one. In that
nothing is my face. A face which is only the trace of a woman
whose name you will never speak, whose house you will
never enter. The wife of an image.

And these pages. They are not discoverable. They are
ruin. A pile of debris along with old boards and the caving
in of a rooftop, weeds and decomposing rats or cats or dogs,
potatoes saved for winter and an overgrown garden. And if
there is water there let it be from a river. And if there is
peace let it be from silence and forgetting. From the slow
settle of dust on a house worn down, on a history lost, on a
woman buried quietly into geography. And if there is memory
let it be disjointed and nonsensical, let it disturb understanding and logic, let it rise like birds or hands into the blood
blue bone of the sky, whispering its nothing beyond telling.
And if there is death then let it be against story, let it ring out
uncomfortably and dull in its terror, let it collect bones like
twigs and hurl them out into space like stars, so that not
even the tiniest escapes constellation, matter, speed.

Let someone lose the captions to all of the photographs;
let them pile into new logics and forms that outlive us.

Trigger/Shutter/Finger (floating)

"Look at his head. Will you?"

"Yes, I see."

"Lolling around on its neck like a child's toy."

"Did you see him earlier? Near the woods?"

"What?"

"He shit his pants. Right in the middle of nothing."

"Filthy animal."

"The thing is, his testicles and privates were…engorged. He looked as if he had elephantiasis or something. Huge and beastly, purpled like eggplant."

"God."

"I tell you, I don't know what we are going to do with these creatures. Their lives devolved to this extent, their usefulness gone. What kind of country can we expect to emerge from this kind of excess rot? Best leave it to nature. Think of them as the rot that produces life. Death regenerates—brings forth new life, like rotten flesh and refuse in a compost heap. Eh?"

"Of course, sir."

"It's an ecological fact."

"Yes."

"I suppose they think of themselves as prisoners, in that self-absorbed and arrogant way. Good Christ, did they think that they could behave in any fashion at all? That they had no responsibility whatsoever? We have an ethics to sustain here, after all. A new society. Every generation of leaders must generate a new society."

"Of course."

"My daughter, for instance. Educated as if she were a man. Brilliant, really. And a real survivalist. Do you know, she is well practiced in the physics of explosives and military strategies? Why, she should have been my son. She would have made a superb son."

7. Photokinesis

Father's Day.
Dearest Michael.
Dear, dead Michael.
No. Victor Gogal. Erik Mikol.
No. Nikolai. Nikolai Dimitri Juknevicius.
She sighs audibly and her fingers dip into her drink. She draws a box around each name. Too made-for-TV movie. Her fingers move to her mouth. John Joseph Juknevicius. She swirls the clear liquid around in its shallow bowl. An olive lolls. She drinks. Closes her eyes. Pictures the box of the white napkin that she has been writing on. The father without a face floats behind her eyes, or there in the dark of a bar, making you think the blue black box of a room is a bruise of memory, making you think the linoleum square box of a floor is as familiar as the floor of your childhood house, making you think history's lost itself to a box of a bar whose name you know better than a father's.

Father's Day in yet another city she pictured might house her. She'd lived in a dozen different cities, always feeling her way for home. Her body wore her life, tiny wrinkles writing time in the face, translucent gray cupping the hollows underneath her eyes, skin sagging at the stomach some, arms thinning. Veins emerging like rivers on the infant-thin skin staring up at her. Her own body the image of the years she had lived. The cities she had inhabited. Lives ago. Or the present.

America was this: a woman moving like an image, a man lost to the imagination.

In the bathroom of the bar she turns the black tee-shirt she is wearing inside-out. She'd spilled something on it. Turning the shirt inside out was nothing. No one noticed. She went back to her table. The thing about being at this bar was that she was not likely to run into anyone she knew, and they had several different varieties of martinis. That was their specialty. And she was celebrating. Anonymity refreshed her. She was celebrating Father's Day. No, not really. She was easing into a new self, she was materializing into the image of a new life through chemical alchemy. And she liked the fact that martinis came with food in them. Olives, onions, lemon peels, fathers, come back to life in little balls, whatever a girl wanted. When she'd come in she'd been hungry. Not anymore.

The Four Egles had blue-black light like a bruise, black vinyl seats, dark red-to-black linoleum floor.

The thing about Father's Day was that she felt all kinds of intricate and overwhelming shit that came from nowhere, or somewhere else, did it come from somewhere? She had no idea. She hadn't had a father since she was a child, and she did not remember that figure at all, only a black and white still shot she'd created a thousand times. She thought about the picture of herself as the child of that black and white image and realized it was overdramatic and weirdly weighted. She thought about trying to describe that picture to some-one, someone there in the bar, someone asking her about herself, trying to meet her, trying to know her, on their way to trying to fuck her. She laughed aloud, because who would buy such a sorry ass story as that, like some made-for-TV movie. She pictured the photos, newspaper articles, artifacts of her past packed away in a box in her closet. All she had of a life with origins.

Drawing on a napkin. Doodling, most people would say. But she's not. She's drawing the heads of anonymous men, various designs, some detail. Heads on a white napkin in a dark bar with martinis in the distance. She brings the glass to her mouth, one succulent gulp, an olive lolling into her mouth and balling in her cheek at the end. She's thinking of photographs. She's thinking of the heads of men. She's making thumbnails of her next subjects.

Another, please.

You got it.

She pulls the manila envelope out of her black leather satchel and places it on the table there with her. A drink joins them. She removes the contents: three 8 x 10 matte black and white photos of a tall man dressed in black, from afar. She studies the photos one at a time, sipping in between. She holds the first olive in her mouth for a bit. How long has it been? A month? Two? She doesn't know.

The first time she saw him he was riding a bike into the horizon, not riding it very well, either, as if riding a bike was unnatural to him. He jerked this way and that on the thing, and it didn't go in a line, but more in little swerving "s" shapes down the road. She'd followed him immediately, as if by instinct, as if her body knew something that she did not understand, and she found herself turning in her car to chase the shrinking man speeding awkwardly away on his bike. At one point she missed a turn due to traffic, and so had to turn at the next street, and the thought of losing him sent an unbearable cold knife into her temple. Her heart raced without permission, her fingers made claws around the steering wheel, and when she finally came around the block and spotted him again it was as if oxygen had been restored to

the world after a short vacuum of unknown origins. She had
not once thought to herself, why am I doing this? She had not
once stopped the car to analyze her actions, to consider in a
rational light what moved her. After all, what is one woman
driven toward a man in the larger history of things?

As always then she fell into a rather precise pattern, one
with logic, sense, and tune. She followed him to and from
work. During lunch hours. At night and on the weekends, in
parking lots or diners, city streets or convenience stores, once
all the way to the next state—a bed and breakfast near the
sea, a woman with him but left out of every shot. She did
once catch a bit of the woman's leg in a photo by mistake;
there it appeared like a severed limb begging attention.

From following him she learns him. His clothes are never
wrinkled. They are the kinds of clothes that she imagines
New Yorkers of his age wear. His hair is black as a record
album, combed back stylishly. He wears black pants, a white
shirt, a black leather jacket. He wears a thick silver necklace
with something she cannot quite make out hanging from it.
And a bracelet, a watch. All thick silver. His shoes are more
expensive than her monthly rent, a detail that endlessly fas-
cinates her.

From looking at his mail when he is away she learns that
the man is either an academic, a freelance journalist, or a
writer of literary works. Return addresses are from maga-
zines and from publishers. Bills are ordinary. Personal mail,
rare. He lives alone. The house is not empty in this way.

Once she takes the mail altogether and reads and reads,
for days she reads, she takes them around with her, she
places them on a table in the bar, she drinks with them, has
whole conversations with them, laughs out loud as if they
share something intimate and profoundly amusing.

When she begins, she begins from a distance. A lens
zooms in on a man who has no notion of the hunger living
with him.

In one image his face is larger than the frame of the shot: facial features bleed beyond their borders, eyes lose their human look and take on the appearance of blurry mouths. In other shots he is an ordinary man; striking. Or moving from one place to another, out of a cab into a building, out of a building into another, out of the world into an image. What is hanging from the thick silver necklace: a hand, a tiny silver hand, palm side up.

Up to one hundred. She would always take up to a hundred photos of them, turn her life in the direction of a single man's story, recorded through image and light and the arresting of movement through a mechanical procedure, a false eye. One hundred. Like a century. All over her walls the man would hang in his various guises, two-dimensionally resolved and given compositions. It was as if she was building a man each time. Nameless, they would take on a narrative shot to shot, frame by frame. As if she could hold the whole of her world in her head, in her hands, a history of images that delivered her.

The accumulation of the black and white stills then came to have meaning for her in a way that nothing else in the world did. No lover, no job, no movement between cities. Piles like ruins of tiny civilizations in wooden crates she'd carried around with her for years. What was she that these were her "belongings," she sometimes wondered. Something like an armed isolate, what might be called a stalker, meandering through the urban territory of sensuous accidents. Where most people have forgotten that the present offers a neverending series of experiences, she lived every moment to excess.

But fuck it. Who was she trying to kid? She knew these thoughts were out of sync, from a history long dead and forgotten. Paul Martin's London. Arnold Genthe's San Francisco. Atget's twilight Paris, Brassaï's sex, Weegee's naked city as obscene disaster. Bruce Davidson's Harlem. Official realities broken down and through with a small black box shooting open a hole. The hidden truth is tantamount to the vanishing past. Good-bye, fatherland.

So she would gather photographic evidence of the life of a single man, trace it, accumulate its images, order and refine them, adjust the light, the contrast, crop the realities down with surgical precision.

And when at last she had the story of a man, she would break into his house and leave him those that most represented his existence. For what a man never achieves in his life is a raison d'être, an image of himself that proves he was alive.

More than anything in the world, more than her own life, she desires to be caught, captured, punished.

In the bar she faces the photos and places her hands over them, closes her eyes. He is more beautiful than is humanly possible, but not in the ordinary way. She takes little time in imagining her next move, finishes her drink, collects the photos, puts her coat on in one fluid movement.

She sits outside, inside of her car all night, a block down from the house that the man entered.

Memories of not remembering anything of one's past come to her. A man and a house, the hands of a child. The black of night, a woman in her car watching. Night develops everything into black and white, shades of gray bridging reality and dream, past and present.

The captions on the photographs are a signal. When we read his name in a caption, it is a signal. Do you understand?

No, he is not dead. But we will never see him again. Think of him ascending like an angel into heaven.

In memory the house is not the house, it is an image, the floors, the wall, the hands, the folds of the brain, gray. The house is the gray of the sky in late afternoon snow to evening white to the cover of night. Or the house is black and white, the girl, the cold white land of a small closed body. The too loud crack of a winter-hit city. The sting of breath in the night, the sweatless body, the mind of a child.

The rooms of a house at night.

In memory nothing is real, the family is not a family, the house not a house, the room a question, the door an opening, a box in the closet not a wooden box but a world between her small hands. A little coffin. Stuffed with photos gray blue sepia black and white nameless faces.

A story of a father taken in the night. A story of a photographer captured and imprisoned. Images replace words.

Many a night she simply sat in the room with her knees encircled with arms and hands, her chin resting on knee caps until shivering drove her back to her own bed and to an unwanted sleep. But always before sleep her mind broke from thinking and into, not dream, but as yet unmade dream, a waking wander back down the stairs and across the wood floor and into the room to the door and the promise of an image on the other side.

A child crazy with desire. Her hands in the wooden box, the touch of longing meeting each edge and slick surface. The smell of chemicals when held to the nose, the taste of toxins to a child's tongue. She has cartwheeled each photo between small hands. She has held an image to the ear, to the nose, she has tasted them with her mouth. She has looked and looked but each time she is looking for only one. One image among forever. One photo dislocated from any history to the hands of a young girl unable to name countries or lines on a map or streets of a city or a father in the house.

Each time she moves through the squares of life in the wooden box she replaces it in a random position, like a deck of cards, like a card trick wherein one is trying to outwit the magician. And each time she comes across the image with new wonder and some terror she can neither name nor suppress. Her hands disappear to the stun of the image in her eyes. The eyes are the entire body in that moment, unable to resolve. It is this: in the foreground, not a man's body and not a woman's body but a body spread across the width of the frame. Unclothed, flesh gorged from genitals to sternum. Head rocked back in horror or mouth opened to gasp or eyes rolled back into sockets. The mouth, or is it a wound, the sex too, horribly open to the eye. The teeth larger than the mouth can contain. The sockets of the eyes blackened and sunken as if the head was an over-ripe fruit. In the background, a dead, belly-gutted horse, its mouth more open than a beast's.

How many times had she thrust the picture back into the coffin and shoved the box back into the closet and pulled old woolen coats over the top of it and shut out, hard, the image and the door and buried beneath her covers in bed...she had cried ceaselessly, or anger, or what? Her face red-hot her body on fire her fists in little knots of white knuckles her unformed pubis stinging. From the first night forward she could not not. There is no longing deeper than a child's.

This night so many nights later she waits for a man to leave his house so that she might enter its dark. This is a wholly different life, she thinks. But her hands betray her. They twitch and tingle with memory.

A woman drives up in a Saab; he leaves with her. It is nothing. The routine of lovers.

She has a black leather satchel with her. The clasps are thick silver. She opens the car door. For a moment she is still there, between being inside the car and outside, between being outside and inside of the house, like the image of a woman who cannot be taken, a photo untaken, black and white. She avoids the front door. She moves to the side of the house; windows are locked shut. She moves to the back of the house. The back door is locked. But there is another door, a deeper one, down some stairs to a basement. She walks down the stairs into black. Her hands find the doorknob. It is not open, but neither is it closed. In a movement of pure force she shoulders into the wood and turns the knob and heaves. Almost masculine. It gives.

She has entered what appears to be a study. A room where he works, writes, something. A desk, computer, stereo. Books line all the walls. They are uninteresting to her. All his furniture is uninteresting to her. She does not want to know a single thing about him beyond his image.

The desk is perfectly empty. She makes her hands flat on the surface of the white desk. She opens the black leather satchel. She removes three photos, all black and white. She arranges them on the expanse of the white table. Each image of him turns, stares, faces her in its frame. The eyes are black. The mouths, hair, black.

She is seated at his desk. She fondles them, one at a time. As her hands find and let go to the eyes, the mind, the knowing, her jaw drops slightly, lips part, her tongue lolling in its house, spit welling. She has learned to look beyond herself. She has learned to leave her body. And yet again, it is the body that overtakes her inside the images. She is holding an image of him laughing up in moonlight. His mouth gaping open reveals a thousand tiny inarticulate shapes and fluids without names. Her hand between her legs working in soft rhythms, mindless or childlike. Not thinking, her head eases on her neck's perch, then slowly, always tethered by sight to the image in her other hand, the image tilts, and retreats, retreats and back and back until the jaw is nearly perpendicular to the face, her head rocked back until the tendons in her neck bulge, her skull locking back away from its neck as the skull with its terrible holes and its blur of a face pulling past human, her hand working and moving. She is shocked out of herself by her own hand. Wet.

She brings her fingers instinctively to her mouth and finds salt with finger to tongue. With her hand in her mouth she returns her vision to its familiar. The photo shakes; a quivering overtakes her.

The photos populate the table. Before she leaves the room she rests her cheek on one small corner of white, flat, like land, like a field of ice in a country, a life, a name she will never know. A man randomly chosen. A promiscuous woman.

Father.

Box (floating)

Wood grain; skin. Form. Gift. Body. Trope.

Perhaps the box is small. The size that one can hold between two hands. Perhaps it is a child holding the box. Perhaps the child brings the box to its face. Smelling. Perhaps the child extends its tongue out to lick the surface. Perhaps the child's hands discover the veneer. In the child's hands the box is an object. What is inside is a question larger than desire, larger than wars waged, larger than death. Who among us can withstand the ache of a child?

Perhaps the box is larger than a body. Perhaps it is a coffin. No question begs amplification; this box is endlessly meaningful. The box the size of a body stands in for all of our lives. We do not need language, nor sense, nor understanding. A head bows. Eyes close. Someone in the room begins a prayer. Another, a song. Someone in the room knows loss. Someone else, grief. The wood sheen shines up like a lacquered truth. This box houses us. This box takes us home.

But the box may not be a box at all, it may be an abstract form or some other architecture larger than a single life. The box may be a house, and in the house a room, and in the room windows or bars or walls or doors and a heart beating inside a rib cage. Is this freedom or containment?

Perhaps the box holds an image, its technology and grammar advancing imagination and light. Box-headed lens-eye duplicating biology. Lens: a grounded or molded piece of glass, plastic, or other transparent material with opposite surfaces either or both of which are curved, by means of which light rays are focused to form an image. Eye: the vertebrate organ of vision having a lens that focuses light on a retina. Panoptical: traversing the seen/scene in a territorialization without limits. Omnivoyeuristic: the power of an outside gaze to invade any and all territories. Camera: an apparatus consisting of a lightproof box having an aperture through which the image of an object is recorded on a photosensitive film or plate.

Perhaps this page, this sentence, all of grammar, an entire lexicon captured or delivered.

8. The Aesthetic Object

Her back is to the box. The box is a wooden crate the size of a person, the height, the width. Don't talk to me about losing faith, she thinks. Wake up, will you? This is how life goes. Alone in a room with a crate the size of a human, all the rooms empty except for the two of you like that. In place of a father. My god. Someone should say something, make a joke, change the subject. Someone should flip the channel, turn the dial; no. There is no *dial* to turn. That is from another time. Grab the remote. Shift the picture endlessly. Channel surf. Get it? Idiot box. She laughs at her own bad jokes.

Pacing her body like a cat's between the crate and the window, her hand moves now and again to her mouth, her fingers move as if they are holding something, her lips twitch some. Focus your eyes on something, you idiot. Do it. She looks at the trees outside of the window. They are birch or something of that nature. She doesn't know trees. But somehow the word "birch" comes. She is focusing all of her sight on those little spindly trees, the whole goddamn row of them. Somehow the word "birch" deforms in her mind's eye into the word "bitch." She has a pop-up thought of the trees bursting into flames, one at a time, like trick birthday candles that won't blow out. She has another pop-up thought of a script memorized from childhood: *The Stelmuze oak is known to every one of our countrymen, young and old. To strangers who do not yet know it we hasten to explain. The Stelmuze oak, about 2,000 years old, stands on a spot in the lake district of Zarasai—that gem of nature in the northeast. The oak is perhaps the oldest extant in Europe. The giant tree that has grown old and for which so long nobody had cared was beginning to ail. But naturalists after the war attended to its wounds, cleared the ground around it and now this fine old oak, its thirteen metre trunk firmly rooted in the soil, is alive again. Every year it is visited by thousands of tourists and we see its image in postcards. The foresters recently planted oak crops from the grandchildren of the old Stelmuze oak. Generations are coming.*

Behind her the crate, watching. The crate, a wooden and dull question. The crate, her life. Her thoughts double and roll. What is a life what is a life what is a life? She leaves the apartment occupied.

Out on the street her legs alternately thrust before her like punctuation thuds or some goddamn thing. Her own shoes disgust her a little. Their price almost as much as a month's rent. When did she become this? The black leather shines terribly up at her. Clicking heels on pavement. Her hands shoved down in the pockets of her coat as if diving toward her own knees. Stop frowning goddamn it. With that jawline, with that blonde hair, those beady little blue eyes, the furrowed brow, you look like a fucking fascist bombshell. Relax your face for christ's sake. She is headed to a flower stand on the corner. She is headed to a Chinese take-out restaurant. She is headed to a little market for wine, candles, matches, plastic cups and plates. She is headed anywhere that will take her away from what has come to her.

Dear Lilian Zitkus:

There is no other way to begin this letter but
with frankness and clarity. We have located
the remains of your father, and, as you are
the only living relative, we would like to know
your wishes. I don't think it will surprise you
to know that there was considerable debate
regarding contacting you at all; some in the
committee felt that this decision was a matter of national history and that the body be-
longed to the country of its origin. Others
thought those family members of the victims
dead at your father's hands ought to have
some say. One member of the committee tried
to destroy the body himself. I hope that his
passions, though misplaced, are understand-
able to you. I assure you we made every attempt to respect your rights and duties.

It is said that Lincoln's body was carried across
the country by train. Somehow people thought
that even in death his body would suture the
wounds of a nation. That it could move a
people to forgive one another like thread traveling to make seams. I do not know what
your father's body will mean to you. I can
only imagine that this is a terrible weight, as
heavy as all of human history, or perhaps
heavier still, a weight unmovable, unbearable, one that wrecks history altogether. I do
not envy you. I send my deepest regrets, in
this case, not for the death of a loved one,
but for the discovery of a body that moved
against humanity itself, and how you must

find a way to carry that body through your
own life. We are prepared to help make any
arrangements acceptable to you. Please con-
tact us as soon as possible.
Respectfully,
Mr. Kosoviz

Guilt? Was this an emotion that had ever invaded her
thinking? Or was it something that had eluded her for her
entire life? She had no answer, the question sat before her
two dimensional as always, black and white, partly ridiculous, hysterical, partly enigmatic, profound, sacred. What
moves us in a single life? When history's face has distorted
far enough to re-emerge as a great, cinematic close-up, when
we've no way of receiving it save pure myopic, imagistic
surrender, what's left? Stop. Stop. You are an idiot. Your
mind is more stupid than is humanly possible. You have a
more exaggerated sense of self than anything American, more
than a Hollywood movie director, than any politician, than
any psycho-killer or rock star or soldier or any male rising
heroically to cinematic glory. You will destroy yourself from
ordinary thought like some fucked-up science experiment
mouse. You have no place in history. You are a daughter.
Rodent. Woman.

Though it is beyond the time of night during which people
ordinarily eat dinner, she will eat dinner on the floor next to
the crate at this time. She opens the plastic bag containing
the plastic cups and puts white tulips in several white cups,
along with some water. They lilt over the sides in small arcs.
She lights one of the candles, white, and drips enough wax
on the wooden floor to anchor it. She holds it there until the
wax dries. She opens the little white boxes of Chinese food
one at a time. White rice. Spicy green beans. Ginger chicken.
She opens the wine, white; she pours it into one of the
plastic cups, toasts the crate, drinks the whole cup down

and pours another in a single motion. She is sitting on the
floor even in her wool suit, a little like a child. Her legs
splayed out as if they are broken.

The shadow from the crate casts itself across her body
like a coffin's. She smiles and toasts the crate. Stop being so
overdramatic. No, don't. Be overdramatic. Laugh your ass
off. There is no rule book for this. There is no way to suc-
ceed or fail. She thinks, you are your father's daughter, you
are sitting on a hardwood floor of an as yet unfurnished
apartment with a box filled with remains, a box that has
traveled an untrammeled geography, born into your life without permission, origin, or grace. The bastard's home.

Chewing a mouthful of food as if it is the most normal
thing in the world. She stares at the crate, its wood grain
coming clear in the candlelight, then receding like a past
into dark. She finishes the bottle of wine, enough so that her
eyesight fuzzes over some, the wood of the crate, the wood
of the floor, the wood of her brain all bleeding over into
each other. Thoughts dull as tree branches criss-crossing.
She forgets what's what.

She takes off her blazer. She removes her skirt. Her blouse.
White silk falls to the floor like some secular surrender. She
slides her thumbs underneath the waistband of her pantyhose
and inches them down over her own hips, her ass, her thighs,
bunches them down over her knees, her shins, her ankles,
sits on the floor, scoops them free of her feet. She removes
her panties. Her bra. She is a naked woman alone in a room.
No, not alone. She walks across the wood floor to the wooden
crate. She presses her breasts and belly against it. She closes
her eyes. She breathes. She places her palms shoulder-high
against the crate. She ties her pantyhose around and around
her head until she is blindfolded. Then she feels the wood.
Strange Braille. She smells the wood; oak. She touches her
tongue to the surface of the crate, then harder, until she
hitch-catches splinters on the thick wet flesh. Her brain like

twirling knives. Her tits hardening against the wall of the wood. Her hips pressed in so that the bones double grind into the wall of it. She inhales deeply. And when she exhales, she pisses down her own legs until it pools there on the wood floor.

In Washington, DC there is a library containing atrocity files, trial records, documents and videotapes and recordings and disks and microfiche, artifacts of events, markers of dates and times and identities collected and organized in some great historical pile-up. Miles of information accumulated in site-specific fashion, so that a person might hold the evidence in their own palms, so that judgments might be made, so that questions might be answered, so that stories will not be lost, so that memory might outlive slaughter. So that *victims* might be counted, *monsters* punished, *crimes against humanity* brought into the light and burned from existence. In this library an exhibit fills the lobby, so that visitors will have an entrance marked by the emotive power of the events or people they wish to track. One would not, after all, want to enter the library without some deep sense of the historical weight of the material contained inside. One would not want to dismiss the *horror*. One would not want to disown the *tragedy*. One would need to enter the library in a frame of mind owing to the severity of the facts. After all. The library contains the *evidence* of *atrocity*. The *actual documentation*.

The exhibit includes objects behind glass. For instance, gold fillings in a pile the size of a bed. Half murdered diaries and journals that have been hidden behind toilets, under floorboards, inside the walls for years and years. Names written but unspoken for years, scratched onto paper still smelling of age and rot and rain and the oils of an ordinary hand. Near dead children's toys, blackened and sick, a wooden horse, a mutilated doll, jacks and a ball. Another pile: children's shoes. It is enormous, this pile of little shoes. Its height reaches the ceiling. In another building, the building across the street, for example, the Museum of Modern Art, it would be an aesthetic object designed carefully, beautifully, its weight out-weighing the facts. But in the lobby of the library the pile of tiny shoes stands like an act of resistance against viewing them. The shame. Every act of seeing a crime. Every tear. Every walking away to view the next glass encased horror of biblical—or cinematic—proportions. *Suffer the children.*

But children today are watching television and blowing each other to bits on video screens. Their hands accustomed to killing virtual enemies, destroying other races like evil aliens in a moving cartoon. Their thoughts inextricably linked to terminals, networks, systems. The word *war* is a foreign object.

She moved to Washington, DC in an effort to begin from nothing. When she first received the letter, she ignored it. She did not throw it away, but neither did she respond, and in fact she has no idea in hell what she did with it. Two months later she received the second letter, and then a third, and a phone call, a fax, emails, and more of the same. Communications piling up like leaves. It of course became clear to her that they would keep coming, these communications from nowhere, from people she did not know. Like the men that came to her over years and years, these messages would continue. Begging. No matter what her name was in the life she had carved out for herself, no matter what her job, who her friends were, who she fucked or did not fuck, these words were going to invade her life forever. She tried to remember exactly how many people she had lied to about who she was, her family. The stories of her dead father. My father is dead. Years ago. A car accident. A plane wreck. A horrible drowning incident. He was a famous architect. He was a defense attorney for prison reform. No. He was unremarkable in every way. He sold insurance. We were not close. Never once had she said my father the war criminal. The famous. The televised. She tried to catalogue in her mind how many lovers she had narrated her lack of family to. And what they had said. Had they said anything at all? Had they loved her differently?

She takes them to bed exactly the same. Give me your wrists. Your ankles. Give me your ass. The ropes will burn marks into your skin but they will not last long. Have you ever had a fist in your ass? A hand balled into muscle? The wrist twisting up the anal cavity until your mouth surrenders to animal? Have you ever had your pubic hairs burned off with a flame? Have you ever been beaten or marked or struck dumb with pleasure? The whip slap of black leather on white skin? No, they have not, and they do everything she asks, and they lie there ready to be overcome, to give up, they have waited their entire lives it seems, they cry, their eyes wide with longing, their thinking driven out of a skull as if by a single and precise blow to the head. How many times they come.

The gap between the name on the communications, *Lilian Zitkus*, and the many names she has given herself is as wide as a nation.

Her furniture arrives in the middle of the week. She leaves the crate damn near the center of the room, arranges her things around it. She has given herself a month to go to the library. In one month she will force feed herself the knowledge of her father the murderous beast.

The first time she makes the walk from her apartment to the library her feet look ridiculous to her. She thinks, I've changed, these shoes do not belong to me. That day instead of going to the library she detours and enters a shoe store and buys knee-high black leather boots, approximately half of the price of one month's rent. Instead of going to the library she spends the afternoon in a posh bar with a view of the Washington Monument. She drinks Balvenie scotch for five hours until the Washington Monument sags on its axis some. Her feet hurt; the leather is new and stiff. With each step home her toes and ankles burn. But the black sheen of the leather heel toe heel toe hypnotic wet as a blacktop black as that almost blue of night her own legs her own feet overtaking her taking her home. Home?

Thus it comes that she fails to enter the library for the first week.

She begins the next week as if starting over, the way we pretend like the year 2000 is a millennium, she pretends her own personal history begins whenever the plot pulls. This is the first week, she says to herself, as two more weeks go by. Each time she begins again, as if time did not have a reliable pattern, as if days simply piled on top of one another in indistinguishable heaps, so that one could say: "This present never ends, it simply duplicates itself." She thinks of this sentence one night when she wishes someone would take a black and white photo of her boots. Composition. Of course the crate is in the background. She longs for someone who might make this photograph real. There is not a single moment in which she thinks of taking it herself. She's no photographer. Get a grip, will you? Stop pretending to be so dramatic and artsy. But her longing is enough to make spit fill her mouth.

Finally after the first month has passed and the second month has passed and she has begun to wear the same clothes every day, a uniform of sorts, she finds her legs taking her to the library. Almost like an ordinary visitor.

In the first week she learns the posts, the assignments, the ranks. She learns what position he occupied in the order of things. She learns what power he had, the kinds of commands he enacted, military litanies. It is easy, he is not an obscure figure after all, what did you think, that the information would be hidden? Obscured? Lists. She learns that her father reported to only two other superiors. She learns that he had one of his own right-hand men killed for refusing an order. She learns that the order was to sever the arm, mid-way, of a photographer. She does not learn what became of the photographer; the information is incomplete. And this is only one story.

But in the second week she discovers a few pieces of information that suggest her father had further relations with the photographer. She learns that there is a "case number" for this "incident." She finds that there are 1,500 case numbers associated with her father. She feels as if she might vomit, then notices that she is wet between her own legs. She places her hand there. Her cunt is throbbing. She is ashamed, then not. My god. You are a grown woman. Get a hold of yourself for christ's sake. But she can't stop her own mind's walking. The case numbers remind her of economies, of money, of all the ways in which we count ourselves present.

Perhaps because she is tired, perhaps because she has jettisoned what she knows for her entire life, perhaps because she wishes she were someone, anyone else's daughter, a child-beater, a sodomizer, whatever, she becomes obsessed with the case involving the photographer. She becomes so hungry to know she cannot take in any other information or facts about her father. She wants only to know what happened between them, why the incident was assigned a case number, who the photographer was, what her father did to him, or did not do to him, or anything in between. Stories form inside her head in great waves, two men facing off against each other, one with the power to torture, the other with the power to witness. What a crock. History is lost to us in this way. We don't think in these terms any longer. What utter bullshit. The fact is that men no longer find themselves against one another in this way. You should know. More than anything else they need the cunt of a woman, the tits, the mother-loving wide open as a mouth, ass. History is dead except in the body of a woman and a man coming home.

While sitting there in the library going over the documents, viewing the screens, enacting searches, she tears a piece of paper and eats it. She has no idea she is doing this. The taste is oddly familiar, comforting. She puts more paper into her own mouth and eats it. Her throat thickens.

In the third week she finds his name underneath three photographs. Three black and white photos of a tall man dressed in black from afar. In one image his face is larger than the frame of the shot; facial features bleed beyond their borders, eyes lose their human look and take on the appearance of blurry mouths. In other shots he is an ordinary man; striking. Or moving from one place to another, out of a car into a building, out of a building into another, out of day into night.

She has always known his name. The proper name has lodged itself inside language, unmovable, imprinting itself across time and television, anything meant to signal the historic flow of events. The name has outlived every trace, every body, every meaning, the name larger than any life, ballooning out and up black letters on a white page overtaking all of space. In her mind, his name. In her movements, his name. Her body, his name. Her thinking, her DNA, her blood, her bones ringing his name like the bells of a new religion. Her very sex his name. Who among us could untether a self from a name such as that? The perfect domination precisely received.

But in the fourth week there is an interruption that changes the face of her entire life. In the fourth week she finds a different photograph. It is not a photograph of her father. His name is absent, though she finds several conflicting stories that carry the same photo from different angles. It is this: in the foreground, not a man's body and not a woman's body but a body spread across the width of the frame. Unclothed, flesh gorged from genitals to sternum. Head rocked back in horror or mouth opened to gasp or eyes rolled back into sockets. The mouth, or is it a wound, the sex too, horribly open to the eye. The teeth larger than the mouth can contain. The sockets of the eyes blackened and sunken as if the head was an over-ripe fruit. In the background, a dead, belly-gutted horse, its mouth more open than a beast's. The photographer with whom she is obsessed has taken these photos.

It is something like an epiphany, what she feels, some joining of previously untethered logics. One sentence dominates her thinking: *I am my father's daughter.*

Without thinking she Xeroxes a copy of the photograph. And again. Too many times. The same image. Until she has one hundred Xeroxed copies of not the original, but a representation in a book. She thinks of the number one hundred. She thinks of the century. Numbers become black and white images that fill her brain, larger than life.

Sitting there she has a still shot memory of one man from her past. Not her father at all. A lover. He has haunted her, or rather, his body has. It happened in a single moment. His wrists and ankles had been tied, as always. His torso straining against reality. She had been riding him, her head rocked back, her eyes open. His cock stabbing her anus, up her spine. Her eyes closed. She had been fingering her own tits. Suddenly one of the ropes giving way, his hand loose, freed. Him grabbing the ropes winding around his other wrist, releasing himself. His hands around her skull. His hands throwing her tiny head into the wooden wall. Her coming as if death. Her uttering a single word: *father.* Her losing consciousness there, briefly.

When she had come to a few seconds later she heard the words "Baby, are you OK, baby?"

A librarian comes to wake her. There is a little drool between her face and the books she has covered. The librarian saying, "Are you OK?"

Walking home her legs look like sticks to her. Duller than sticks. Stick figured woman useless, being unheard of existence marching leg after leg and again home. Bourgeois idiotic being. Duh duh duh duh duh thudding human. Up the stairs to her door thudding. Opening a glass door opening. To the elevator that is her life rising. To her front door. White on white. White of the eye meeting white wooden door. Her mouth pools with spit. She knocks. Laughs. Opens.

Once inside she immediately removes all of her clothes. In her mind she gets a visual representation of a sentence: we are born in black and white. We are born into representation, into a story that pre-exists, our bodies are useless against this truth.

Somewhere in the history of her body she convulses. Matter released to corporeal spasm. She drools. She touches herself. She comes in a shot in less than one hundred seconds. Little death. She laughs hysterically, like a woman. She doubles over and vomits next to the box. She sits and sits like that. For days. Eventually she shits on the floor.

Tremor. She sees her own hands pitched before her as foreign objects. They work and work. Somewhere in her mind's eye her hands have come to stand in for her whole body. She is naked. She has not eaten for days. She sat on the wood floor staring at the wooden box until she was moved. Her hands moved her, finally. Her hands and the Xeroxes. Each black and white Xerox some kind of proof. Stilled shots. Little deaths. Exactly the same. Never deviating. Endlessly repeated. Perhaps for the rest of time.

She has pasted them on the walls. She has pasted them on the hardwood floors. She has covered the windows. She has covered the door. She has covered the wooden box; it is clothed in Xeroxes like some art object. Centered in the

room. She has covered the bed. The refrigerator. The mirror
in the bathroom.

She has covered the television's glass eye.

She has even covered the oven, inside and out.

Turn the dial.

Fragments from an Unknown Woman (floating)

Fragment from an Attic

Who gives a name? Whoever wears the dress of light. She does not make a sound; a child is sleeping. Soft go the pads of her feet, softer than the breath of history. Silent is the breaking of her heart. She moves toward words as if toward arms hugging a body in shivering cold.

Fragment from the Cunt of a Woman in Love

Ache to the deep center of a place not the spine, but near the spine, bone to flesh to blood to desire. Taking her beyond herself and out of the world toward a spinning or pounding. Death lives careful and tender here. Given over to the torture and heat of flesh to flesh to hip the swells and dips and rise and fall and over. A mouth opening. A head rocking back to its deep internal. Lips suck open, hunger consumes or produces itself in endless waves of hot and wet.

Fragment of a Severed Limb

Carry as if a cradled child to a wood over white, white sand of frozen. And the wind escorts the figure's stumbling, but the arms are perfectly bent and the limb is not to fall. The wood grows slowly, slowly and soft in a blur of vision or sight misted over with almost sleep, almost thought, almost as yet unfinished body inching its way. The wood is black but then is green, and greener through deep toward black in its green as a hole or an eye or the cup of a palm held small enough. The limb is carried into the wood, out of wind, out of white into thick of dark and the soft underfoot of needles and shrubs and dirt, and the bark like skin on each body of tree surrounding and taking and hugging the figure, the limb. The forest does not echo.

Fragment from a Universe Without Order

Who took the corpses from the fire, ash? Who lifted bodies not to heaven, but to the ordinary day? Who formed words and sentences into stories that broke time and reoccurred at random? Whose grief spilled to joy and everlasting? Who swam in the sea until salt disintegrated to formlessness and motion and blue, whose tears endless, whose face as a cool pool of longing?

Fragment of Alone

The back, its body cracked at the cusp of spine and hope, is not broken. She is unbroken.